Raven Cove Mystery

A Rinnie of Alaska Adventure
Book One

Halene Petersen Dahlstrom

Publication Consultants

PO Box 221974 Anchorage, Alaska 99522-1974

ISBN 1-59433-001-8

Library of Congress Catalog Card Number:
2003108911

Copyright 2003 by Halene Petersen Dahlstrom
—First Edition—

Manufactured in the United States of America

Dedication

This book is dedicated to my family—
Dan, Jeff, Kati, Colter, Jennalee and
Danny—who have been so devoted to
me during this writing project. Your patience,
input and support make this dream of mine
possible. Love ya tons!

This book is also dedicated to anyone—like
Rinnie Cumberland—who cares enough to
reach out to others, and is willing to stand up
and be counted for good.

Table of Contents

Acknowledgments

Many thanks to the great family members and friends who helped with details, served as cheerleaders, or read manuscripts at various stages for me throughout the writing process, especially Joel'lene Anderson, Thera Bagley, Bob Baer, Merrell and Nadene Dahlstrom, Rachael Cartwright, Dr. Ilona H. Farr, Dottie Grimes, editor Marthy Johnson, Harriet Petersen, Lois and Evan Swensen, and The Red Hat Society.

A Note from the Author

Every morning I look out across my back yard and see a beautiful Alaska lake. So many times I've wished that I could share the scene with others—especially those who might only be able to read about it. Searching for a way to introduce the great Alaska outdoors to youthful readers, I began to wonder...

What if there was a tree house in my backyard?

What would I be able to see from up there?

What would I hear?

What would I smell?

What if I was alone up there one morning when something unusual happened and I was the first one to see it?

What would I do?

How would I feel?

But since I'd have trouble getting into that tree house, I decided to create a character who could climb it for me—probably a girl—since I'm still one at heart.

How old would she be?

Eleven's good.

Twelve, maybe? No, I've done that before.

What about thirteen, about to step onto the roller coaster of teenage life?

Yeah, I liked that. It seemed to fit, and sparked my imagination.

The next question was: Just who is this girl?

And suddenly an answer came...

Chapter 1

The Tree House

Rinnie Cumberland snuggled further down into her sleeping bag, pulling the dew-dampened pillow in with her. She loved sleeping outside in the summertime, except for the wet-pillow part. Then again, there was the shivering-shocks part that hit her body when she had to leave the warm sleeping bag to rush through the wet grass and crisp Alaska morning air to get to the house for the bathroom. It was that call of nature that had awakened her, and Rinnie knew it would be impossible for her to stay in her cozy cocoon much longer.

Mom had warned her about taking the big Tupperware container of black cherry Kool-Aid out to the tree house. But Rinnie had wanted to thoroughly enjoy the experience since it didn't happen often, and her family celebrated just about everything with black cherry Kool-Aid.

The tree house was her brothers' usual hang-out, but they were off to scout camp for ten whole days. Alright! Russell and Squid wouldn't be too happy when they found out Rinnie had taken their spot almost as soon as they left. Mom didn't mind her having a turn, but she'd had a fit at first about Rinnie sleeping out there alone. Thankfully, Dad had won the air horn argument.

During his freshman year, Squid had bought the air horn to blast enthusiastically when the high school teams scored points. It was tolerated at the football games, but it had become an absolute no-no during basketball games ever since a startling sudden blast made the high school principal dump his root beer all over the school superintendent. Since then they'd sneaked it into games, used it quickly, and hid it under someone's coat to keep from having it confiscated. The perturbed principal would spend half the game peering hawk-eyed through the crowd trying to spot where the noise had come from.

That loud, annoying noise made the air horn very useful to Rinnie. Few kids she knew of were allowed to sleep outside alone in Alaska unless they had a well-fenced yard or a mother with nerves of steel. Rinnie had neither.

"What if a bear comes through the berry patch?" Ruth Cumberland had protested. "Or a moose? Or even worse … a stranger?"

"We haven't had a bear out back since we quit filling that dang bird feeder, or leaving scraps out for Rascal. We live on the outskirts of town, not a bar within six miles, so that discourages wanderers. But either way, if Rinnie gets concerned, she just has to trumpet that horn and we'll come a-runnin' with the shotgun," Bill Cumberland answered in a teasing-heroic way. "I'm more worried that she'll be eaten alive by mosquitoes!"

Rinnie was too, actually. But the first hatching of monster mosquitoes, Alaska's unofficial state bird, was over, and the second batch of smaller, meaner ones didn't seem to like the evening breeze off the lake or the bug repellent she doused herself in, so that was good.

The conversation had gone back and forth for several minutes, with Dad coaxing, "Besides, hon, it barely gets dark enough to sleep outside at all. She'll probably lie awake all night wishing for a moose to walk by just to keep it interesting. Or she'll give up and come inside to her room so she can pull down the blinds and actually sleep."

Mom reluctantly gave in.

Snuggled down in the sleeping bag, Rinnie knew that was true. Alaska June nights rarely get dark enough to require a flashlight outside except for reading, which is just what Rinnie had done until very early in the morning, drinking Kool-aid and munching graham crackers. From the outside, the tree house looked like a miniature cabin on stilts. It had a sturdy sloped roof and two cut-out windows, one on either side, so you could look toward the lake or to the backyard and the house. The walls enclosed it only three-fourths of the way around so it sometimes got a bit drafty. Rinnie was prepared for that, though. Her brushed-flannel robe was tucked into her pillowcase to wear over her summer pj's if she got cold.

On the front of the tree house a wobbly rope ladder hung from the open balcony. There was room for three kids to sleep, but her brothers were always trying to cram a few extra friends into it, creating more weight than the structure was meant to hold. Then Dad would have to say, "Okay, boys, you know the rules," and make some of them sleep in a tent on the lawn.

The tree house was the hub of activity for the neighborhood boys, but the quality of the construction and all the nails that were visible showed that it was a beginner's project. Luckily for the boys, Home Depot had a 5-gallon bucket of camouflage-green paint on their rejected-paint sale. The only other choices left had been pale yellow or lavender. Rinnie couldn't help thinking about how funny it would have been to see her brothers with a lavender tree house. But regardless of the color, she was grateful now that they'd finished it.

The first thing Rinnie did to establish temporary ownership was to tack up a long string inside each window. From each of these she hung an old pink towel that Mom had donated for curtains. It was an awesome addition and gave the place a nice rosy glow when the sunlight shone through. The perfect atmosphere, and such a fun place to hang out, read, or just think. Without the tree house, there was nothing for her to do.

Her friend Erica was on vacation, having a great time at a family wedding in Idaho, then going to Disneyland. Other friends were busy with visitors, or in summer school, and the girls' camp-out with her church group wasn't for another month. Rinnie might even have appreciated playing with her mother's finicky cat, Miss Tizzy, if the darn thing hadn't disappeared a few weeks back.

"I've heard eagles snatch up and *eat* cats or little dogs," Mom had remarked sadly.

Dad matter-of-factly chimed in, "It's more likely that she's been grabbed by a fox or a coyote."

Mom hadn't found much comfort in this.

With nothing special to do, no friends to call, no brothers to bug her, library books were her only escape from the reality of her boring life. It made her happy at least to have a turn in the tree house.

She loved looking out through the trees at the lake below. When the summer sun and rising moon shyly danced across the sky, they painted the lake in beautiful colors. Golds and blues in the morning. Silvery pinks in the twilight hours. In fall and winter the colors were even brighter, like electric rainbow sherbet. Rinnie loved living under such gorgeous Alaska skies.

The Cumberlands had lived in their hand-me-down house on the ridge above Raven Cove

Lake for four years. It was an old, in-need-of-repair place, and sort of embarrassing next to the nicer houses in the area, but it felt like home, and it had a great view of the lake. It also had plenty of neat big trees. From up there, Rinnie could see most of the Raven Cove area.

Many changes had taken place since they'd moved there. Most of the little homestead cabins that had been scattered around the nearly two-mile-long lake were vacant now. A developer, who was going to sell lots to rich people with floatplanes, had recently bought them up. Rinnie wasn't happy about that.

Around 3 a.m. Rinnie dozed off, only to be awakened a couple of hours later by an annoying squawking bird.

"Caw, caw," it called.

Groggily, Rinnie tried to convince herself that the bird noise wasn't unusual. After all, ravens, eagles, ducks, loons, geese, grebes, seagulls, magpies, and chickadees were often around in the summertime. Occasionally even a swan could be seen out on the lake. The loons were her favorites.

But the cawing didn't sound familiar and seemed to become more urgent. This caught her attention, and once her brain was fully awake, her bladder sent a telegram. Rinnie tried to ignore it as long as possible, not wanting to crawl out of the warmth of her

sleeping bag only to get chilled to the bone
by the time she reached the house. She
stalled, trying to force her mind onto the
otherwise peaceful morning.

When a breeze drifted through, she could
smell the flowers her mom had growing
around the yard. The delicate iris and lily of
the valley scents were almost overpowered by
the luscious perfume of lilacs and Sitka roses.
Adding to the fragrant feast were the blooming
mountain ash and crab apple blossoms from
neighboring trees, along with a variety of
bushes that grew down the hill between the
Cumberland's house and Mr. Moore's.

Mr. Moore was a nice old man whose sweet
wife Greta had died a year before. They were
like adopted grandparents to the Cumberland
kids, especially to Rinnie. Greta had even left
instructions in her last will and testament that
Rinnie be given her treasured collection of
Hummels. Rinnie hadn't been in a big hurry to
go get them. It would have been too drastic a
change for Harold. Besides, Rinnie could see
the twelve precious figurines whenever she
wanted. The Cumberlands checked on Harold
Moore every day, took dinner to him, and
helped him with his medicine. That is, until
three months ago when his sister-in-law Magda
moved in to take care of him. Then things
changed. Now wild raspberry runners, alder,
and fireweed were starting to camouflage the
little path that ran between the two houses.

Rinnie wriggled uncomfortably. She would have

to make a bathroom run soon. She wasn't sure what time it was, but figured if she was quiet going into the house, she could hit the bathroom and then go back to sleep in her own bed before Mom woke up and started thinking up creative tasks for her to do. That sounded like a good plan. Boys have it so easy, she sighed. They can just go in the bushes.

Caw! *Splash!*

Now a splash? wondered Rinnie. The fish in Raven Cove Lake weren't big enough to make *that* much noise. "It has to be my imagination," she mumbled to herself. The big fish were out in the rivers or the ocean, not in little lakes like this. But the splashing grew louder and the cawing much fainter.

Her curiosity finally won. "Oh, all right," Rinnie groaned out loud and began unzipping and untangling herself from the sleeping bag. The chilled air hit her, just as she was afraid it would, so she grabbed her robe and reached for her slippers. Dang it! She'd forgotten to put her slippers into the bottom of her bag to keep them warm and dry. Now they were damp and cold. Oh brother! Bare feet on the wet grass would guarantee frosted tootsies as she ran to the house, and add to her misery, so damp slippers were better than nothing. She slipped them on.

Rinnie turned quickly and peered through one of the

cut-out windows of the tree house. Wait! No. It wasn't a bird call. It was a crying out—like a voice in dismay.

Then she saw it. A canoe drifted about thirty feet from shore and someone was hanging onto the side of it with one arm and thrashing the water with the other. The call came again. She had to do something, and fast!

Rinnie looked around, grabbed the air horn and pushed the button. A rude blast shattered the morning air. She pushed it again, then scrambled down the unsteady rope ladder. Within seconds, both of her parents came running out of the house.

"What's wrong! What's wrong!" Dad yelled, as he hopped his way into a pair of jogging pants, a rifle under his arm.

"Rinnie! Rinnie! Are you okay?" Mom exclaimed, not far behind him.

Rinnie ran a few steps across the lawn toward them. "Someone's drowning in the lake! Hurry, Dad!"

Bill Cumberland dropped his gun. "Call 911!" he hollered to his wife, and headed down the weed-choked path.

With his long runner's strides, Dad didn't need Rinnie blocking his way, so she ran behind, getting whipped by the wild berry branches he'd stirred. Still she followed.

"Stay here!" Dad yelled when he reached the end of the little boat dock. Then he dove into the water. Rinnie stood there watching—her heart pounding. She anxiously listened for the sound of sirens in the distance. Then the shivers hit.

Chapter 2

Unanswered Questions

As she served a late breakfast, Ruth Cumberland wondered aloud, "What was an 80-year-old man doing on the lake at five in the morning? It makes no sense! Where was Magda? And where was Rascal? I've never known that dog to leave his side."

Rinnie sat wrapped in a quilt at the kitchen table. Despite a long, hot shower, her teeth were still chattering. "D-didn't D-dad t-tell you?" Rinnie stuttered. "She w-was sitting on the p-porch step w-with a br-broken ankle, couldn't move."

"Oh, honey, listen to you! Here, have some more hot chocolate and get warmed up. Your oatmeal and cinnamon toast are coming right up."

Freshly dressed after his shower, Dad came into the kitchen. "That shower felt much better than that cold dunking a while ago!"

"Thank heavens for hot water," Mom added.

"Amen to that," he agreed with a chuckle, then

bent down and kissed the top of Rinnie's head. "Quite the little hero we have here."

Rinnie shrugged, her hands wrapped around a big mug of hot chocolate. "Y-you w-were the one who jumped in after him. I just h-helped him up onto the dock."

"Just? That was a big help! And you had a robe you could wrap around him. That helped a lot too. It was all I could do to get him to let go of the canoe. He didn't recognize me or trust me at all at first. He was so out of it."

"Didn't recognize you? After all these years? That's very strange. And what's this about Magda? She broke her ankle?"

"Yup. Says she was going to take a shower before Harold woke up. When she got out she noticed that the door was open. She looked out the window just in time to see him trying to get into the boat, and went running out to get him. Unfortunately, she tripped on that lopsided step, broke her left ankle and couldn't get up. They took her in the ambulance when they took him."

"That's weird."

"Real weird," Rinnie mumbled, feeling a little warmer, but very troubled.

Something wasn't right about the whole situation, especially the way Magda had acted after they'd fished Mr. Moore out of the lake. Rinnie had run to the Moore house to get a blanket. She was the one who'd found Magda sitting on the step. Funny thing was, the woman didn't seem distressed. Sure, her foot was hurting. It was all puffy. She told Rinnie it was broken. There were some scratches and slivers on her face as well, but she wasn't crying or carrying on about Harold at all. When Rinnie told her they needed a blanket for him, Magda said, "Well, I am certainly in no position to go get him one."

"That's okay. I can," said Rinnie and side-stepped quickly around Magda, and was into the kitchen, before she heard Magda protest, "No. Don't go in!"

Rinnie had spent plenty of time there before Greta died and knew her way around the house well. She looked in the hall cupboard where the quilts and blankets had been kept in the past. It was nearly empty. None of Greta's brightly pieced quilts were in there, just a couple of well-worn blankets and an afghan. Rinnie grabbed them all and ran back out. As she stepped around Magda again, she wrapped the afghan around the injured woman's shoulders. Magda actually scowled at her! Rinnie hadn't expected to get hugs and kisses—it was no secret that Magda didn't like her—but she might at least have been grateful. Still, Rinnie didn't waste too much time pondering it right then. Getting the blankets to Harold, who was in shock, was her priority. She helped Dad get the confused elderly man wrapped up, and since they could hear the ambulance getting closer, they sat him down outside in his favorite wooden lawn chair. He used to sit in it a lot, Rinnie remembered. But it had been ages since she'd even seen him out of the house. Rascal, Harold Moore's mixed-breed pet and sidekick was nowhere to be found.

She was explaining about Magda's where-abouts when the ambulance arrived.

"Okay, go check on her again, Rinnie. Tell her they'll come help her next," Dad directed.

Rinnie was glad for that instruction because she had an urgent need to go back to the house. The bladder telegrams were coming about every two seconds. Out of breath from running back and forth, Rinnie relayed the message. "Good news! The ambulance guys will be here to help you in a minute," she panted, trying to appear hopeful and helpful. "I hope you don't mind, but I hafta use your bathroom!" Rinnie again started to step around miserable Magda.

Roughly, Magda grabbed Rinnie by the leg. "I *do* mind! You should go home now."

Rinnie was ticked. She'd rather be home. She'd rather be home in bed! She definitely needed sleep. She was freezing and wanted to cocoon herself inside her flannel patchwork comforter. But what she needed even more right that minute was a bathroom!

She jerked her leg away from the woman's

grasp. "Sorry, I can't make it home!" she said and ran into the house again.

When Rinnie came out of the bathroom, she was greatly relieved. First, for the obvious reason, and second, because the EMTs were taking care of Magda out on the step, so she didn't have to deal with the grumpy ingrate anymore. Rinnie paused in the living room, waiting until they had the stretcher in the ambulance. She could hear Magda talking about how she was *so* sad about Harold's mishap, *so* worried because she'd called and called for help, and *so* appreciative that some-one had finally come. It was so phony it made Rinnie sick. Sighing and frustrated, she glanced around. What she saw next made her even sicker. The living room was practically bare. The TV was missing. There was no ste-reo with its record collection. No end tables with homemade doilies under little pots of violets. No polished burl lamps. Even the cute pillows and the matching afghans that Greta had crocheted were missing from both the couch and Harold's old recliner. Those were the only furnishings left in the room.

The fireplace mantel was vacant. Only a ghostly outline of the display case where Harold Moore kept his favorite pocketknives, could be seen on the wall where the case had hung for years. But what stunned her the most made her heart nearly stop. The bookcase where Greta's precious Hummel collection had once been so proudly displayed was empty. Rinnie stared in disbelief.

"The lady wants us to get her purse and lock up now," an EMT called out from the kitchen.

"Oh, okay," was all Rinnie said. On her way out through the kitchen, she made it a point to glance at the different spots that Greta had once decorated with pictures or knickknacks. She really wasn't surprised to see them missing, too. She shook her head sadly.

"Are you okay? You look a little pale." the EMT remarked, as she walked past him and out the door.

"I'm just real tired."

"Maybe we should get you checked out at the hospital. Been a pretty stressful morning for you. I heard that you were the one who saw the old guy in the lake and got some help. Good going!"

"Thanks, but I just need to go home." Rinnie started to smile, noting how cute the guy was, even though he was way older than she—like in his 20s. Then it dawned on her—she was in her pajamas! Her face turned bright red, and she took off running for home.

———

As she sat drinking hot chocolate, and thinking about the bizarre happenings of the morning, Rinnie grew increasingly worried about dear Mr. Moore.

"Yes, it's awful how fast he's gone downhill in

the last few months. He was always so sharp, so independent." Mom added. "Maybe it's a good thing that his sister-in-law came to stay with him. She's just going to have to lock the doors at night so he can't wander off."

"That's for sure!" Dad said, recalling what he'd been told. "She said she had no idea that he was in the water until she heard him splashing. All she could do is sit there and holler in hopes someone would hear her. It's good that they took her in the ambulance too. Gonna check them both out."

The telephone rang and Dad went to answer it.

Rinnie looked up thoughtfully, holding a spoonful of oatmeal in midair. "You know, there's something about Magda and her story that doesn't make sense."

"What do you mean?"

"Well, for one thing, there was only one voice calling for help and it was coming from the lake. Also, her hair was dry and there was no steam in the bathroom like after someone's had a shower."

"With all the excitement, how can you be sure?"

Rinnie was about to say that she was very sure. She wanted to spill the beans about all the odd changes she'd seen after making her bathroom run, talk about all the missing items that used to be in Harold Moore's house. But

29

just then Dad came back into the kitchen and the subject changed.

"Speaking of excitement, they just called from the newspaper. They want to take a picture of Rinnie in the tree house to run with the rescue story."

"Oh, how nice!" Ruth Cumberland exclaimed. "We'll have to get some copies to send to all the relatives."

Rinnie nodded and smiled at her mother's enthusiasm. She was still bothered by the Magda mystery and the state of things in the Moore house. But she was also a little worried that her brothers might not think it was so great that Rinnie had been up in their tree house, and a picture would just be proof.

Chapter 3:

Too Much to Think About

That night Rinnie slept in the house. She needed to be able to pull down the blinds in her room, snuggle under her comforter and shut the world out. Still, she tossed and turned all night and woke up more tired than when she went to bed. Her brain was hyperactive, but her body was going in slow motion, and after she washed her face that morning, Rinnie grimaced at herself in the mirror. She didn't know what to think about herself.

Half the time she liked the way she looked. Half the time she didn't. She knew she wasn't ugly, but wasn't considered super-cute either, just as average as any 13-year-old girl could be. Almost as tall as her average-sized mom, Rinnie occasionally worried that she'd get a growth spurt and end up as tall as her dad, and have to look down on all the boys the rest of her life. She wasn't dumb and could do a lot of different things fairly well, but nothing remarkably well. So why pull a face? Well, for one thing, her hair was annoying. Why had she cut it? Her long, light-brown hair had been easy to take care of all through elementary school. Then some teen magazine article said cutting it would make you feel more fashionable and grown up. But it didn't.

It was getting more and more complicated to be a girl. Even being average could be overwhelming sometimes. Today it was all too much. And what about this hair? She couldn't wait for it to get down to her shoulders again so she could throw it into a ponytail with a scrunchie and go.

"Hey, kiddo, hurry up! Your French toast is getting cold."

Rinnie pulled another face at herself. French toast. See? Even her breakfast was average! Oh well, it was food. Rinnie shrugged and dragged her tired carcass to the table.

Her mother seemed to notice that she wasn't exactly zipping around full of energy. Maybe that's why after breakfast she didn't reorganize all the cupboards and put new lining in the drawers, a project she'd wanted Rinnie to help with. Instead she brought in two baskets of towels, socks, and miscellaneous things for Rinnie to fold while she herself sorted though the spice cupboard and talked to a lady on the phone.

Mom knew when not to push too hard. She was the kind of person everyone liked and lots of people confided in. Rinnie used to talk to her all the time. They still talked, but never really got into the kinds of things Rinnie would have liked to talk about. Dumb timing because at 13, Rinnie had more things than ever that needed talking about. Stuff that was going on with her. Stuff she worried about. Not that Mom didn't try.

She was a born-again-Oprah kind of lady. Years earlier Ruth Cumberland had quit watching the daytime talk show because the content was inappropriate and mind-numbing. However, when she heard that Oprah had changed her show and was now encouraging people to read, get involved, exercise, and truly communicate, she had rejoined the ranks of true followers. Rinnie, who'd plop down on the couch with homework and work hard on it during the commercials, usually ended up seeing more of the show than her mom did, though. Poor Mom always had interruptions of some kind—phone calls, boys squabbling, or dinner or laundry to check on. Still it was amazing how many Oprah-isms and strategies she picked up from it.

It wasn't uncommon for Mom to work interesting questions into the conversation when she and Rinnie were busy doing things or driving places. Are people bugging you to do drugs? Have you read any good books lately? If you could be anything in the world, what would it be?

Rinnie always said no to the drug question— she knew that junk was available at school, but kids knew that the group she hung out with didn't do that stuff, so she usually wasn't

hassled. It was easy to name a book or two—
she'd always enjoyed reading. Answering the
what-do-you-wanna-be question was much
harder. There were a lot of things she considered becoming. She was afraid some of her
ideas might sound silly, so she didn't let herself go and blab a lot about them, like she
used to do. Why, she didn't know. It's just the
way it was, one of her gnawing, new regrets
about her relationship with her mother.

Sometimes Rinnie thought Mom deserved a
better daughter—maybe one who would be
enthusiastic about making cutesy table settings
for holidays, and putting out the good china
on Sunday. It wasn't that Rinnie didn't like
those things. She just didn't like them enough
to get all psyched about doing them.

She was aware, too, that her mom would've
loved to do some of the major home decorat-
ing she'd seen on TV. The old house could use
a makeover. But the money just wasn't there
for that extravagance. Keeping their house
came first.

When Dad's Uncle Jay died a while back, he'd
left a big old house by Raven Cove Lake, and
a monstrous pile of medical bills. Rinnie's
family was doing okay, but lived in a tiny
house with no room for a family of five to
grow. They had a family meeting and decided
to take Uncle Jay's house and add on an extra
mortgage to pay off the medical bills.

Mortgages were a mystery, but what was clear

to Rinnie was that their house payments were high and there was no money for much else. Her parents worked hard and they had what they needed. Both worked for the school district during the school year. Dad taught high school geography and coached track. Mom worked in the office of the junior high as an attendance clerk. In the summertime Dad drove a tour bus. Mom used to work at Carr's in the bakery, but since she'd been put in charge of the women's Relief Society at church and people called her all the time about things, she'd decided not to work this summer. It was neat having Mom around home. It meant that the boys didn't rule the roost, and there were better dinners at night. But that also meant there wasn't much in their activity fund for anything extraordinarily fun, and sometimes extraordinarily fun sounded so appealing. Oh, well.

Her mother looked over at Rinnie as she hung up the phone. "Well, I guess they're going to keep Harold in the hospital for tests. He's malnourished and very low on his thyroid. Magda will stay for a couple of days too. Apparently her blood pressure was very high. But her foot isn't broken. Just a bad sprain."

Rinnie didn't say much. She was interested in the part about Harold, glad he was getting food and treatment. But Magda—well, she'd have to figure out how she could keep an eye on her.

"Have you heard from Erica lately?"

Rinnie jumped, startled out of her deep thoughts. "Uh, yeah. Got a little card yesterday. I forgot to tell you about it, what with the photographer coming and all."

"Are they having a nice time?"

"Yeah. Erica liked being a bridesmaid for her cousin. But she had to wear some kind of horrible lime green chiffon dress and there were bees buzzing around her flowers. Other than that it went fine."

"It was nice of her to write."

"Yeah, they are probably at Disneyland now." She sighed again.

"Lots of people go to Disneyland every year. They get to see other people in animal costumes, a replica of the Matterhorn mountain that's 50 years old, less than two hundred feet high, made of metal, plastic, and painted-on snow. They spend lots of money, and get into big traffic jams going and coming. Gee, sounds fun to me!" Ruth Cumberland smiled sarcastically.

Rinnie knew what Mom was trying to do, make her admit the advantages of living in Alaska, where with a short drive you could see real animals in the wild, or wait until one ran down the street. And where mountains, like McKinley, were over twenty *thousand* feet high, and had glaciers *millions* of years old. The worst traffic jams happened when people were trying to get to the river to fish. Alaska was great. They'd moved there when she was little and she couldn't really remember living anywhere else. Yet there was this yearning for other things and other places. Still, she could play Mom's game.

"Yes, but Alaska doesn't have cotton candy and snow cones."

"In the spring and summer it does. Just go down to the Saturday Market."

"And what about the rides?"

"We get carnivals in town several times a year, and at the State Fair in August. Then there's the day tour stuff. But maybe the Dumbo ride sounds more interesting than say, a boat ride out to see whales and sea lions. Or riding a snowmachine across a glacier."

Rinnie smirked. "Speaking of boat rides and snowmachines, there's plenty of stuff in Alaska to spend money on."

"Yes, very true. But there are plenty of things that don't cost a lot. Hey, Disneyland isn't exactly cheap either!"

"True, but what about the Mickey Mouse hats?"

"Rinnie, would you honestly *wear* a Mickey Mouse hat? I think we can probably find several shops downtown where you could buy a moose antler headband if you really want one. Then you can call yourself a moose-keteer."

Rinnie laughed. "That's okay. But that reminds me, we haven't played tourist for a long time."

"Yeah, we need to do that again soon, maybe when Dad goes to pick up the boys from camp. And speaking of rascals, ha ha ha, you like how I worked that in? I was thinking that someone ought to check on Mr. Moore's dog."

Rinnie chuckled. "That was smooth, Mom. I'll go look for him; take him some of that Meow Mix we have."

Ruth's smile faded with the mention of the cat food. Rinnie could have smacked herself for mentioning it and spoiling the lighthearted mood. The gray Persian's disappearance was obviously still a tender spot on Mom's heart. Now it was her turn to sigh, but soon she tried to smile again. "Sure. Might as well use it up."

"Do you think I should go look for Rascal now?" Rinnie started to get up from the cloth-ing-piled table.

Ruth chuckled and shook her head. "Nice try—but I don't think Rascal would mind if you finish the folding and put it away first."

Chapter 4

Tug-Of-War

After lunch, Rinnie wandered down the hill behind her house, jumped the ditch, and crossed the road to Mr. Moore's house. She could hear a dog barking far away, and she hurried to the lake side of the little house. In the distance, along the shore to her right, someone was shouting and tugging back and forth with a dog over a shiny blue object. It looked like a kid. It also looked like Rascal. Might as well check it out, Rinnie thought, and headed along the shoreline.

The boy in the tug-of-war was about Rinnie's age, a little taller, and the blue, shiny thing was a remote-controlled boat.

"Let go, you dumb mutt!" the boy grumbled, his full concentration on the determined animal.

"Drop it!" Rinnie commanded.

The boy dropped his end of the boat, startled, and the dog ran about ten feet away with it, and started to chew.

"Is this your dog?" the boy asked, exasperated.

"No. He belongs to my neighbor. Haven't seen him around for a while. He looks awful! I've never seen him this skinny."

"He's been hanging around the construction site for almost a month, they said. The workers have been feeding him lunch scraps, thought he was a stray. I didn't think so because of the tag on his collar. But nobody could ever get close enough to check it out."

Rinnie walked toward Rascal. He moved off another few feet. Pulling the baggie of cat food from her pocket, she tried to tempt him. "Come on, Rascal. You don't want to eat that icky old blue thing! I've got something for you."

Rascal came closer, sniffing as Rinnie shook the food out onto a flat rock. Then he dropped the boat and pounced on the food, eating fast and wagging his tail. Rinnie patted his back softly. Even slight pressure seemed to make Rascal wince in pain. "Poor little critter! Wonder what happened to him? It's so unusual for him to wander from home," she said, as she handed the boat apologetically back to its owner. "Sorry about the bite marks."

"I think it's fixable," the kid said with a smile. "I couldn't believe he attacked it like that. He just came out of nowhere, swam out and grabbed it. I've been following him for quite a while, waiting for a chance to get it back."

Rinnie laughed. "Beats me, why he'd do that.

Maybe he was just desperate for something to eat. He should be okay now. Anyway—hi, I'm Rinnie Cumberland. I live up the hill over there, behind Mr. Moore's."

"Oh, I heard about you. You were in the newspaper today."

"I was?"

"Yeah. 'Teen's Quick Response Saves Neighbor.'"

"Oh—that." Rinnie suddenly remembered the reporter she'd talked to and the picture by the tree house. She felt self-conscious. "I didn't think they'd get it into the paper so fast."

"Good job, though. Wow!"

"Just a lucky coincidence. I heard something and looked over by the lake and—well, it was my dad who actually dived in to save Harold."

"Still, that was pretty cool!"

"Thanks, "Rinnie said, moving a couple of rocks around with the toe of her shoe. There was an awkward silence for a moment, then she looked up. "So, who are you?"

"Oh—duh, sorry," he said, and smacked himself on the forehead. He waved his hand slightly, "Hi! I'm Nicolas Nedders. I don't live here. Just come and hang out sometimes when my dad has work at the site." Now it was Nicolas' turn to be embarrassed.

Rinnie tried not to smile, but failed. "Hi."

Moving the conversation along, Nicolas pointed to the center of the lake where Mr. Moore's canoe was adrift. "Is that the old guy's boat?"

"Yeah, but we can't get it until my brothers bring our canoe home from scout camp. My dad didn't feel like another swim just yet. That water's pretty cold. Besides it's drifted a lot farther out now."

"I could bring my dad's little boat tomorrow and help you get it in, if you want?"

"Hey, that would be cool. Do you live close—" Rinnie stopped. *Nedders*. The word recognition hit her brain. *Nicolas Nedders*. His dad was the developer who was buying and selling the lots around the lake. Now Rinnie wasn't sure if she wanted anything to do with this kid.

He didn't seem to notice her turmoil, and kept right on talking about how he was sure his dad would let him bring the boat for such a good cause, and he could meet her by Mr. Moore's dock in the morning, if she wanted to ride with him. Then they would go out and tie a rope to the drifting canoe and tow it back for the old man.

Rinnie was studying the situation while he rambled on. Here was this guy—pretty much an average kid—kind of funny, almost cute, a little nerdy in a sincere sort of way. He prob- ably didn't want to come off like he was begging, but he must have been bored silly since coming to stay with his dad, who was obviously busy with the lake development project. Maybe Nick was glad to finally meet someone near his age who wanted to do something. Anything! He was trying to be so nice. True, his dad was not one of Rinnie's favorite people. Actually she'd never met the man, but she was very upset about the changes being made at Raven Cove Lake. Still that wasn't Nicolas' fault. She could see how the canoe rescue might be helpful, and it might get her out of matching another basket of socks all morning, or cleaning out the refrigerator with her mom. So she nodded. "Okay. So what time do you want to meet?"

Nicolas seemed relieved and excited. "Is ten too early?"

"No, probably not. I just have to check with my mom, but it should be okay."

"Cool! I'll see you then, Rin—it's Rinnie, right?"

"Yeah, are you Nick, Nicky, or Nicolas only?"

"Whatever," he smiled, shrugged, then walked a few steps.

Rascal started to growl and slink forward like he was getting ready to attack the boat again.

"Rascal!" Rinnie scolded and slipped her fingers under his weathered leather collar to keep him in place at her side. "Leave the boat alone. Besides it won't taste as good as you think."

Nicolas laughed. "Thanks. So, are you gonna take him home?"

Rinnie nodded and petted the old dog again. "Yup, I'll take him. He and I are old buddies."

"Cool! Okay, see you tomorrow."

"Bye, Nick." Rinnie said, trying not to let on that she thought this guy was rather interesting, nor paying too close attention to him as he walked away, even when he tripped on a rock. But the second time he tripped, she couldn't help but giggle.

"Come on, Rascal. Let's go get you something better than cat food."

Chapter 5

Memories

At dinnertime Rinnie told her parents about the changes she'd discovered at the Moore house, and explained about finding Rascal, starved and bruised. Her parents exchanged worried glances. She knew their concern. How do you go about being a good neighbor without being considered just nosy? If you make a pest out of yourself, they're not going to like you. They may even come to hate you. But if you don't get to know anything about your neighbors, then how do you know when to reach out and help? Rinnie sat quietly, pushing the last four bites of pork chop around her plate slowly, rearranging the green beans. She missed Greta.

Greta was such a sweet little lady. She was the first person who'd been friendly to them at church and in the neighborhood. It was easy to like her, to love her like a grandma actually. Harold Moore was a little tougher to get to know. He kept to himself at first until he got used to the Cumberlands and their noisy brood. He let Rinnie's dad and the rambunc-

tious boys keep their canoe at his launch. He
talked a lot about his early days in Alaska, and
when he fought in World War II. Harold loved
to tell the story about how his pocketknife had
saved his life. Rinnie knew the story well—had
listened to the retelling of it more often than
her brothers. This had endeared her to both of
her neighbors, and she suspected that she was
their favorite visitor.

She stopped in nearly every day to say hi.
She'd worn a little path between their house
and hers. Sometimes she'd find them sitting in
the yard, Greta reading to Harold because his
sight was failing. He could see most things,
but fuzzy, and he couldn't really read at all.
Sometimes she'd find them listening to the
news, or singing along with records from their
huge collection in the quaintly decorated
living room. When Greta got sick, Rinnie and
her mother fixed dinner for them, then Rinnie
stayed and washed the dishes. Sometimes, ever
so carefully, she dusted Greta's beautiful little
Hummel collection.

"All those will be yours soon," Greta had told
her. "I know you'll take good care of them for
me. I've already talked to Harold and he
agrees that you should have them. Maybe one
day you can use a few of them to help pay
your way through college. Some of them are
from a long time ago, and quite rare."

"Wow—oh my gosh—that's like way too much
to give me."

Greta frowned a little. "I thought you liked them."

"Oh, I do! Tons and tons!"

"Well then, who better to care for them? I used to fuss over them like they were my children, with no other little ones in our home. But since I met all of you Cumberlands, it's been more fun to share. You are like family now."

Rinnie giggled. "Hearing our constant commotion, did it ever make you glad you never had kids?"

Greta leaned in close and whispered, "Well, maybe not boys."

They laughed for quite a while over that, then Greta got serious again. "So, will you take care of my Hummels?"

Rinnie nodded, trying not to cry. "Thanks a lot—wow! But you don't need to give them away right now. You'll feel better soon, wait and see," Rinnie reassured her, trying to be positive, but they both knew it was only wishful thinking.

One day Greta asked Rinnie to get a large, very fancy candy tin out of her bedroom closet. "It's full of love letters," Greta had explained, with a twinkle in her eye. "I'd like to tell you about them, if you care to listen."

"For sure!" Rinnie said excitedly and pulled a chair up close to the side of Greta's bed.

"This is my once-upon-a-time Cinderella story, without the glass slipper. My Prince Charming didn't come on horseback; he came in the mail. I was a lonely young woman in Germany, who wrote to a lonely young man in Alaska every two weeks for three years. I fell in love and agreed to marry him before I'd even seen his face."

"Really? That's so romantic!"

"Yes, I was one of the blessed ones, though. Not every story like this has a happy ending. Not everything people write in letters is true in person. I was only 19, and he was twelve years older. My family members were very unhappy about that, and unhappy with me for going to America and staying in faraway Alaska, especially my little sister."

"Wow, that would be tough!"

"Yes, that part of leaving made me sad too, but it was the right thing for me to do. And lucky for me, Harold has always been a good, kind man." Greta chuckled. "The hardest part was reading Harold's handwriting! Just see for yourself."

Greta showed Rinnie some examples. They were very difficult to read. "At first I wondered if he'd written them while riding on the back of a dog sled."

Looking at the penmanship, Rinnie thought that made perfect sense. The sentences were half written, half printed, sometimes sprawled all over the page, and other times bunched together. At least Harold Moore signed his name the same way every time; the only legible letters were the capitals H and M.

"It used to take me hours to translate them, but I didn't mind. I could tell there was a good heart behind the tumbled thoughts."

Rinnie giggled, "How could you tell when he proposed?"

"Because in that letter, there was money for a ticket!" Harold had sent for her to come to America, and after much prayer and with great faith, she'd gone to meet him. "You take these, Rinnie dear. He will never look at them again, and maybe someday you will write a story about our love."

"But Greta, you may want to read them again."

"If I do, I'll know where to get them," she'd said, and kissed Rinnie's cheek. Six weeks later Greta died.

———

The nightly routine was the same for a while. Rinnie and her mother took dinner down to Mr. Moore. Rinnie stayed after to wash dishes and straighten up. Harold asked Rinnie to please not take the Hummels yet. He wanted everything left as it was. Said it made him feel closer to his wife.

"No problem," Rinnie had told him. "I'll just come and dust them for you, okay?"

Sometimes they sat out on the lawn in the rugged wooden chairs and watched the changing sky reflecting in the lake, and talked. Thanks to the big variety of birds around the lake, there was always a creative chorus of bird warbles, peeps, trills, and squawks to listen to. Often Harold would go through his war stories again, especially the pocketknife story.

"It was the day after we landed on Utah beach in Normandy. I volunteered for a patrol inland. When our patrol came out of the hedgerows and started filing across a field, a German 88 artillery crew spotted us. They sent a round at us and it landed about twenty yards away. The point man and patrol leader, good buddies of mine, were killed instantly. The last thing I remember was how the concussion knocked me off my feet and it felt like a sledgehammer smashed me on the top of the leg.

After I came to, it hurt so bad I was afraid to look—thought my leg was gone for sure. I was so relieved when I finally reached down to make sure my leg was still there. That's when I discovered that a piece of shrapnel had struck my pocketknife—a Case Circle C— that my father gave to me before I went into the service. It left an awful nasty bruise and made it hard to walk for several days. But a medic who checked it said if it hadn't been for that pocketknife, it might well have severed an artery and I'd have bled to death before help arrived."

Rinnie always answered the same way each time she heard the tale. "No wonder that knife's so special to you."

"Dang right!" Harold always replied. "That's why I put it in the center of the knife case, and as soon as I could, I had the dent straightened out of it, and bought a real nice pearl handle for it. I've got others that are worth more in dollars, but the one that saved my life means more than all the rest."

Sometimes, after dinner, Rinnie would read the newspaper to him or the scriptures. Often she'd take the stack of records he'd listened to the night before off the stereo, put them in their album covers, and put on another stack.

"Want Frank Sinatra tonight? How about Louis Armstrong? The Ray Conniff Singers? Mormon Tabernacle Choir? Julie Andrews, or Tennessee Ernie Ford?"

Once she got his preferences selected, she got them all set up so he could enjoy them as he dozed off to sleep.

———◆———

Then Magda came. She called from the airport one day and said she'd come "to help out as only family can."

Harold was uneasy, but tried to be pleasant.

"Do you even know her?" Rinnie had asked one evening as they sat out in the chairs visiting.

"Well, somewhat. She's been here two or three times. Greta seemed to enjoy that, but she was always glad when the visit was over. Magda was only 10-years-old when Greta left home so they were close, but didn't have a lot in common."

Rinnie wondered about that. If Magda was so close to Greta, why had she waited to come until after Greta died? And of all the life stories Greta had told Rinnie, very seldom had she mentioned even having a sister. Still, Magda seemed nice, so Rinnie decided to give her the benefit of the doubt.

Then the changes began.

Dinner deliveries from the Cumberlands were the first thing to go.

"Thank you so much for all your effort, but I can cook for us now," Magda reassured Ruth Cumberland. Every day she spent hours cooking and singing in the kitchen, although— Harold joked to Rinnie—for someone who cooked all day; there wasn't much to show for it at suppertime. He still appreciated it when Rinnie brought her mom's cookies or homemade rolls to share with him.

The next thing that was eliminated was Rinnie's Hummel dusting. "No need to trouble yourself, dear. I can take care of it."

"But I don't mind doing it."

"No, you're our guest. You should relax when you are here, and not worry about a thing."

"Well, I noticed that Harold's medicine is getting low. My mom could get it refilled for you."

Magda's jaw muscles tightened. Her smile seemed frozen or painted into place like on a mannequin's face. "No, that's okay. I need to go to the store anyway. You just run along now."

Rinnie's reading to Harold seemed okay, but anytime they just sat and chatted Magda seemed to be annoyed. Rinnie could tell when she was standing at the window listening by the way the curtains moved. Eventually she just started coming out to change the subject, saying things like: "Oh, Harold, you should see what they are showing on the TV." Or, "There are too many mosquitoes out here. Come in and I'll make you some hot chocolate. Come on, come on. I won't take no for an answer."

There was a tension in the air that Rinnie didn't understand. Within a month there was another big change.

One night as Rinnie was walking up the path toward home, Magda passed her coming from the other direction. She didn't say hi or bye, hardly looked at Rinnie at all, just smiled that odd smile of hers. She'd been up to visit Ruth

Cumberland, and when Rinnie entered the kitchen, Mom sat her down and said sadly, "Magda thinks that maybe you shouldn't visit so much. She thinks you and Harold talk about Greta too much, and it keeps his grief stirred up. She doesn't want you to go down there so much, give them some space, time to heal."

"I don't believe it! It's not coming from Harold at all. It can't be! He says my visits are the highlight of his day. He loves to hear about school, and the goofy things Russell and Squid do. We don't talk about Greta all the time, but sometimes he needs to. He misses her something awful!" Rinnie commented in protest.

"I know, but that's what they want apparently, for a while anyway."

"Well, I don't think that's what *he* wants. She's a really bizarre person, Mom. Harold is not exactly comfortable around her either, and he always seems hungry."

"But maybe he needs a chance to get used to her cooking. He is going to need more help as time goes by and she seems to be trying."

"So how long am I supposed to stay away?"

"For now."

"For now—like until further notice?"

Ruth Cumberland nodded sadly.

"Well, that's dang crappy!"

"Rinnie—don't say that!"

"Well it is! I'm just supposed to not go there anymore? Who is going to tell Harold so he doesn't think we've abandoned him?"

"Magda will explain it."

"Yeah, I bet she will. And I can only imagine what she'll say.'" Rinnie shook her head, then rushed off to her room and cried.

———◆———

Now as she stirred her dinner around and thought about all the changes at the Moore house, Rinnie knew that staying away had been a big mistake. Her parents must have wondered too. Rinnie filled her fork full of green beans and gobbled them down. "I think I'll give the rest of this to Rascal," she said, and left the table. As she whistled and called for Rascal on the back porch, she could hear her parents talking about all that she'd told them. Rinnie was glad they were concerned too. She didn't want to be the only one worried.

Chapter 6

A Hairy Scare

While Rascal was finishing off her dinner, Rinnie wandered out to the tree house to straighten things up. Normally she would have hung her sleeping bag over the rail to air out the morning after she'd slept in it, but things had been so messed up the last couple of days that she hadn't bothered. Still it needed to be done. Besides, she wanted to get the library book she'd left up there, and bring in the empty Kool-aid container. Sleeping out there again that night didn't sound too good—maybe she would, maybe she wouldn't. She was bummed out and didn't feel like being alone. Besides, Mom was planning to make cookies later, and nothing could keep Rinnie away from that.

Gathering up the plasticware she chucked it over the tree house rail onto the lawn, then stuffed the graham cracker wrappers into her pocket. A rope ladder wasn't something you easily maneuvered with your hands full, and the library book was enough to carry. She decided the radio could stay up there one more night, and after hanging the air horn back on its nail, she lifted the bottom of her sleeping bag above her head to shake it.

Suddenly something hairy attacked her ankle. Rinnie screamed.

She dropped the bag and frantically shook her foot. Whatever it was clung to her shin under the sleeping bag.

"Hey, what's going on out there? You okay?" her dad called from the porch.

"Something bit me, Dad! And it's hanging on my leg!"

With her parents coming on the run, Rinnie took a deep breath and in one big yank jerked the sleeping bag over the edge of the rail. Then she gasped and started to laugh.

"What is it? What is it?" Mom cried out.

"It's your lost cat!"

"What?"

Dad looked up at what Rinnie was holding. "Correction," he said, "It's your found cat. And a very fat one!"

"For sure!" Rinnie nodded. Then she handed the tense, hissing creature down to her dad, who passed it immediately to her mother.

"Miss Tizzy!" she cried. "Where have you been?"

"Eating balloons, I think."

"You're right about that, Dad." Rinnie giggled and tossed the library book down to him, then started down the ladder.

"That's absurd! Why would you think she'd been eating balloons?"

"Because she's about ready to pop, dear."

Ruth Cumberland held her precious cat out at arm's length and looked at its swollen belly. "Why, Tiz! You naughty girl!" she exclaimed, and then began laughing herself.

As they walked toward the house, Dad patted Rinnie on the shoulder and said, "Well, kiddo, she's got her baby back. Guess you and I are stuck making the cookies."

Rinnie patted him on the back and said, "Yeah, it's a tough job. But somebody's gotta do it."

They laughed about the hairy scary cat attack episode while making the snickerdoodles and chocolate chip oatmeal cookies. But Rinnie was still quaking inside. She tried not to let on. It was no big deal. But it definitely answered the question about whether she'd be sleeping outside that night—no!

Chapter 7

The Canoe Rescue

Just before ten the next morning, Rinnie left her house, crossed her back lawn, veered right just past the tree house ladder, and leisurely strolled down the path to the Moore house. It used to be an obvious trail, but an Alaska summer has so much sunlight, plants can hit a growing frenzy. In several places raspberry runners and devil's club snagged her pant legs and sweater. Mom had suggested that she take a sweater, in a way that really wasn't a suggestion but an order. Now, Rinnie was glad it was getting snagged rather than her arms. She swatted the fearsome feelers aside. Raspberries were a nuisance, until it was time to eat them. Then yum! Finally she reached the little road behind Harold's house, and passed the side of his shed and carport. There, waiting right on time, was Nick Nedders. His dad's little boat, it turned out, was a nice jet boat, and after that revelation came the sight of Nick's other guest.

"He just jumped right in when I got here," Nick said, when he saw Rinnie's bewildered look.

"Rascal! I wondered why he wasn't around for the breakfast scraps this morning. Silly dog."

Nick laughed and shook his head, "He ate the Egg McMuffin I bought on my way over here, so he's not hurting too bad."

"Well, he's not getting the c-o-o-k-i-e-s I brought," Rinnie added, as she stepped carefully into boat.

Rascal looked up and barked.

"Oh no!" Nick laughed again. "He can spell too?"

The rest of the canoe catching went just fine. But something was very odd. There were no oars in it. Harold wouldn't go out onto the lake without oars. She thought about mentioning it to Nick, but didn't know him well enough to share her suspicions. He might think she was weird. Twenty minutes later, the canoe was tied safely back to the pilings of Mr. Moore's launch. Rascal jumped out, swam to shore and ran toward Rinnie's house.

"He must smell those food scraps."

"Yeah, probably." Rinnie smiled. "Thanks for your help."

"Sure."

"Soooo, uh, well, I guess I should go."

"Okay."

Nick steadied Rinnie's arm as she got out of the motorboat. He started the motor up again, then turned to wave.

"Hey wait," Rinnie called out suddenly, even startling herself. "Umm, I didn't give you your cookies."

"Oh yeah. The cookies."

She handed the plastic-wrapped goodies to him and smiled.

"Homemade? Cool!"

"Yeah, they turned out okay. Me and my dad made 'em last night."

"Wow."

"Well, thanks again."

"No problem. Maybe you could go for a longer ride sometime if you're not busy."

"Yeah, that would be cool."

"Yeah, so let me know."

"Okay, "Rinnie said, and turned to leave. Then she turned back. "I'm not real busy right now. I could go for a little while. My mom knows where I am."

"Alright!" Nick said with a big smile.

Rinnie took off her sweater and tied it around her waist. Nick helped her back in the boat. They started to cruise around the lake, or tried to. Within a few minutes the boat sputtered a couple of times. Nick nervously smiled. Clearly he'd driven a boat before, but his reaction to the unexpected didn't raise Rinnie's confidence in him very much. Then the boat did a terrible thing. It shuddered twice and died.

"What the heck!" Nick exclaimed, and exchanged surprised glances with Rinnie for a few seconds. He really had no idea what to do. He tried starting it three or four times, but it became obvious it was only running the battery down; which they both knew wasn't a good idea.

"Is it flooded?" Rinnie asked, unsure if the problem was with the motor or the navigator.

Nick looked embarrassed. "I'm not sure." His dad had told him things to do in case of this problem or that problem. Sadly, Nick hadn't really paid attention. Now he couldn't remember which thing to do in case of what. He began to look through the glove compartment and on the ledge under the dashboard for a boat manual. It held almost everything you could think of except a boat manual.

Finally he said, "If it's flooded, I think we're supposed to let it sit for a few minutes."

Rinnie's eyes widened. She could just see it

now—Dad comes home from driving the tour bus, and has to come out in a canoe to rescue his daughter, who is stuck in a motorboat that doesn't work. Hmm.

"Cookie?" Nick offered, trying to ease her obvious distress. "I made 'em myself."

"Yeah, right!" Rinnie laughed, and took a cookie out of the baggie she'd put them in.

"So, okay, tell me about *Rinnie*. I haven't heard that name before."

"You haven't? Don't you just have tons of girls named Rinnie in your school?"

"Hmm. Let's see. About twenty Jennifers, ten Ashleys, and a bunch of Jessicas. But no Rinnies."

"There aren't any at my school either."

"What do you mean?"

"At school they call me by my real name. Lorinda."

"Oh. That's a— that's—well, that's a different name too," Nick stammered, then snickered.

"Yup. And too hard for a 2-year-old to pronounce. When I was born, my older brother, Squid, called me Rinnie, and I've been stuck with it ever since."

Nicolas about choked on his cookie bite.

"Squid?"

"Yes."

"You're kidding!"

"No. It had something to do with him being the first baby my dad ever saw delivered, and how when he was born he weighed 7 pounds and was 23 inches long, and when my mom asked, "What does he look like?" My dad said, "He looks like a squid!"

Nicolas burst out laughing. "But a squid is kind of squirmy and slimy and red."

"Yup, you pretty much got the picture. I guess it was one of those, you-had-to-be-there moments. Anyway, his real name is Bill Jr. after my dad. But we've always called him Squid."

"And your youngest brother is Shrimp?"

"How'd ya guess? No, he's just Russell. Named after my uncle. And I am Lorinda Ruth named after my mother, Ruth Lorinda. So, what else goes with *Nicolas*?"

"A nightmare—connected to a lot stranger name than yours!"

"Really? Like how?"

"It started with a war."

"What?"

Nicolas sighed. "Okay, I'll see if I can summarize it. My mom wanted a girl so she could name her Alexis Alexandria Merrimont after her great-great-grandmother. Her sister was pregnant too and wanted a boy. But my aunt, mom's sister, had her baby first and got a girl. So she took the Alexis Alexandria name first. My mom was really ticked and didn't even go to that baby's christening. A month later when I was born and not a girl, my mom took the name of Nicolas, just to get even, because her sister had originally wanted to use that name. But my dad wanted me to be called Trevor. So that's how I ended up with Nicolas Trevor Merrimont Nedders."

"Okay, you win! So, how did the war end?"

"My grandpa got real mad, said that enough was enough, and then we moved. Now they just laugh about it, sort of. My mom never got a girl and my aunt named her next baby Nicolas anyway."

"Adults can be so immature!"

"You're telling me!" Nicolas said, and tried to start the boat again. No luck. "Maybe just a little bit longer. This is the first time it's been run this summer. It should be okay soon." He really wished he could remember what his dad had told him to do in a case like this.

Rinnie's face showed her disappointment. She knew Mom could probably see her sitting out on the lake from the back deck, but she was going to be later getting home than planned and hoped Mom wouldn't be ticked.

"So your brothers went to scout camp, huh?" he said, trying to ease the tension.

"Yeah, have you ever been in scouts?"

"No—we moved around too much."

"Oh."

The conversation paused. They both pretended to look at the scenery.

Rinnie wanted to ask Nick how old he was, but since nobody under sixteen wants to be reminded that they're not sixteen yet, she needed to be creative. A few minutes later she casually asked, "So, do you have your driver's license?"

Nick smiled. "No, not for another year and a half." He teasingly asked, "Do you?"

Rinnie giggled. "Yeah, I got mine last week."

"You're kidding!"

"Of course I am! I've got a year longer than you to wait."

"Okay, so if you could drive anywhere right now where would it be?"

"Disneyland! My best friend, Erica, went to

Idaho for a wedding, then they are going to Disneyland. Now that's what I call a vacation!"

"You live in Alaska, and you want to go to Disneyland?"

"Yeah, I know. My mom said the same thing. Mostly I think I'm bored because we haven't had a family vacation for a long time. I mean, we do go fishing a couple of times a summer, but that's pretty much it."

"Really? What did you catch?"

"Salmon mostly. Kings, reds, sometimes silvers."

"No pinks?"

"Yeah, sometimes. But we don't usually keep those."

"How come?"

"Because there are better kinds. The kings, the reds, and the silvers."

"Well, they sell the pink kind in cans in stores."

Rinnie grinned. "Yeah, but to an Alaskan, eating a pink is like eating a carp in the Lower 48."

"Really?"

"Yeah. The kings are a blast to catch, but the reds taste the best I think."

"How big do the king salmon get?"

"Mine was only thirty pounds. But my Dad got one that weighed sixty."

"Wow! Even thirty pounds is unbelievable where I come from, let alone a sixty-pounder!"

"They're hard to get in! You have to keep reeling and reeling, and there are so many people at the river. You have to yell, 'Fish on!' and then try not to cross lines as you walk down the bank, until the fish gets tired enough to pull in and grab with a net. It's a good thing that you can keep only one a day, 'cause it wears you out!"

"That's amazing! My dad promised to take me halibut fishing in a couple of weeks. Man, I hope he can get away, 'cause I wanna go so bad!"

"I think I would get seasick going for halibut. But I sure like to eat it. My dad's boss gave us some that he caught two weeks ago. We had the best fish and chips!" Talking of food make her stomach rumble, so Rinnie decided to change the subject.

"So, you're from California, right?"

"Well, I was born in Texas, then we moved to California later, when I was four."

"A Texas boy, whoa!" Rinnie teased.

"Okay. What do you mean by that?"

"Nothing. Sometimes people from there have an attitude about it being the biggest state in the United States. My cousin Scotty especially. They forget that they are the *second* biggest. We have to keep him humble by threatening to cut Alaska in half and make Texas the *third* biggest."

Nick chuckled. "Oh. So he's a jerk?"

"Mostly just spoiled. But he gets even; reminds us that he has gone to places like Disneyland and Hawaii. He gets to come up here next year." Rinnie rolled her eyes.

"Oh, great!"

"Yeah. So you lived in California too. How many times have you been to Disneyland?"

"A bunch," Nick said, with a sad grin.

"Didn't you have fun?"

"Usually, except for the last time. At first it was great! We went on all the rides as much as we wanted; bought souvenirs; took pictures with Mickey Mouse, the whole shebang. My folks had been fighting a lot so it was nice to have a day when they got along so well."

Nicolas' smile faded, and he began fiddling with something on the dashboard.

"So what made it so bad?"

"It was bad because it was a phony setup. The next day my Dad left. It was supposed to be temporary, but I wasn't stupid. I've spent the last three years being with Mom for eight months, then being with Dad for four. Now that he's all settled up here and has this big project going, Dad wants me to stay for school."

"That would be cool!" Rinnie blurted out, then back-pedaled a bit. "I mean—uh, what does your Mom say?"

"That's what we're waiting to hear about now. Hey, you want another cookie?"

"Sure." She took the cookie, then pulled on her Henley sweater and fastened its three buttons. The "partly cloudy" day the weatherman had predicted had turned into "definitely cloudy" in the last half hour. Bless her smart mother! "Hey, Nick, I'm real sorry that I said—"

"It's okay. Anyway, that's why I hate Disneyland."

Rinnie nodded. "Well, I don't get to go there anyway. Just hang out with my folks, and sleep in my brothers' tree house until they get back and have a fit about it."

"The tree house sounds fun."

"Maybe you could come see it sometime."

"Sure. That would be cool. Let me know when

you're not gonna be busy. I have to come back tomorrow with my dad. Is that too soon?"

Nick must be as bored as she was. Still he didn't act like he was just desperate for company. He already felt like a friend. "You could come over about three o'clock," she offered.

"Three? I get here about ten."

"Sorry, I have a camp meeting from ten to one and after that my mom sometimes likes to go shopping."

"Scout camp?" Nick teased.

"Ha ha! No, girls' camp with my church group. I get to go next month. It's going to be lots of fun. We make things, cook things, and go hiking. Last year we even went panning for gold."

"Interesting camp."

"Well, it wasn't an official activity. During free time when the leaders were having a meeting, a bunch of us came up with this brilliant idea to pan for gold. So, we got the spaghetti strainer the cook had, and went down to the creek. When the leaders came back, we were all standing in line waiting to filter our handfuls of dirt to see if there was any gold. But we—"

"That's it! That's it!" Nicolas shouted.

Rinnie was startled so badly she nearly jumped overboard. Had he gone nuts?

Nick saw the panicked look on her face. "No, no, no. Don't be scared. My dad told me what to do if I had trouble with the boat. But I couldn't remember what he said. Then when you were talking, it hit me— check the inline filter. He said, if you can't smell gas, it's not flooded, the fuel line might be blocked. Now I just have to clear it and that might do the trick."

"Really?"

"Yeah!" Nick just about hugged her, but caught himself. "Hang on. Okay. Do you smell gas?"

Rinnie sniffed the air in different directions. "No."

"Me neither! That's good!"

"Okay."

Nick began talking himself through the steps his dad had said to take. "Find the inline fuel filter. There! And then detach. Hey, look in the glove compartment for a screwdriver, okay?"

"Sure." Before long Rinnie found a metal, 10-inch box with four assorted sizes of screwdrivers in it.

Nick hummed to himself happily as he unscrewed the hose clamps, then unhooked a tube. "Hold these please," he said, handing the clamps to Rinnie. "We sure don't wanna lose 'em." Next he tapped the tubing on the side of the boat to loosen the junk up. "Now I've

Halene Petersen Dahlstrom

gotta blow it out." He looked at Rinnie and
winced, "This might not taste good."

Rinnie winced too, empathizing. A few deep
breaths later, Nick stopped and looked into the
tubing again. "Hmm, there's still something in
there. Hand me the littlest screwdriver, okay?"

Rinnie quickly responded. Carefully Nick
moved the little Phillips around in the filter,
then repeated the blowout process. "Looks
better!" he said, encouraged, and began reat-
taching. That done, Nick turned to her, "Okay,
let us pray," he said, only half-kidding, and
crossed his fingers.

Rinnie chuckled, but she'd been silently praying for over an hour! Praying for the motor, for
those clouds overhead not to start pouring on
them, and that her Mom wouldn't be upset that
she was later than planned.

Nick had to try the starter three times before
the motor came alive again and they were
headed back to shore.

"Hey, thanks," Rinnie said, as soon as Nick tied
up on the little dock so she could get out.

"You're welcome. Sorry about the boat mess-up."

"Like it was your fault!"

"Thanks for not freaking out on me out there."

"Well, I came close a couple of times," Rinnie

75

chuckled, embarrassed. "But it was for a good cause. I am sure that Harold will thank you too, as soon as he's better."

"Yeah, that's kind of a weird thing to happen." Rinnie leaned forward, ready to confide in him. "You have no idea how weird! Hey, can you safely leave this running a minute? I want to show you something."

"Sure, Nick said, and hopped out of the boat.

Chapter 8

The Porch Discovery

Rinnie started walking toward Mr. Moore's house. "You seem like a smart guy, so let me ask you a question, okay?"

"Uh … okay."

As soon as they reached Mr. Moore's porch, Rinnie pointed to the crooked bottom step. "Can you tell me how someone can run *out* of this house and sprain their left ankle?"

Nicolas looked at her funny. "Why?"

"Because Magda said she got out of the shower, noticed the door was open and ran out to find Harold. But she said she tripped on this bottom step, broke her left ankle—but actually it was just sprained—and she couldn't move."

Nick looked at the angle at which the bottom step was slanted; walked up and down them twice and then said, "Yeah, maybe. But you'd have to hit it just so."

"Okay, but then she had slivers on her face too. The only way she could have gotten them is if she fell—"

"Forward going *into* the house," Nick finished her sentence. "Otherwise she would have hit little rocks on the sidewalk, not the slivers from the porch."

"Exactly!"

"So, why would she say she got hurt going out, when it happened coming in?"

"I am beginning to wonder if she took him out there in the first place."

"Took him? Why?"

"I don't know, but I'd sure like to find out. He'd never have gone out in the canoe alone. Hasn't done that for years."

"And if he had, he wouldn't have gone alone without paddles."

"So you noticed they were missing too? Alright! And, in the house, lots of stuff is gone—just about everything nice—plus Harold's knife case, and all of Greta's Hummels."

"What's a Hummel?"

"You don't know what a Hummel is?"

Nicolas shrugged. "A car?"

Rinnie snickered and continued explaining as she walked away. "No, smarty! It's an expensive porcelain figurine. I'll show you a book about it tomorrow, okay?" A few steps later she realized that Nick hadn't followed her and she was talking to herself. He stood transfixed, looking into the kitchen window.

Rinnie started toward him. Suddenly he yelled, "Run!" and jumped off the porch. He grabbed her arm and pulled her away from the house with him.

"What is it? What is it?" Rinnie asked, breathless, when they reached the boat dock.

"Just the scariest face I've ever seen in my life!"

Rinnie froze. "Oh, my gosh! Magda's home already?"

"Must be."

"Do you think she heard what we were saying?"

"With the look she gave me, I'd say that's a yes."

"Uh oh, that's not good."

"Yeah. She was not happy. I'm getting out of here. See you tomorrow."

"Okay. Hey, thanks." Rinnie waved quickly.

"Sure." He smiled from the boat as he left.

Rinnie started across Harold's yard but stopped as she passed the shed. She could hear growling and whimpering. Rascal?

She pulled the door open just as Magda reached the shed coming from the other direction. In a flash Magda used her crutch and weight to pin Rinnie flat against the open metal door. She could hardly move or breathe. Eye to eye, Magda spat out the words, "You'd better mind your own business, little girl! You don't know who you're messing with. I won't warn you again. Do you hear me? Do you understand?"

There was a scrambling noise and a crash. Suddenly Rascal ran out of the shed. He nipped Magda's shin just above the ace bandage that held the splint on her sprained ankle. "Ow!" she cried out, releasing her grip to swat at the dog. Rascal and Rinnie ran through the yard, across the road, jumped the ditch and scrambled up the hill as fast as they could go. Rascal dove under the Cumberlands' back deck to hide and Rinnie ran into the house. Mom was on the telephone talking to another troubled soul. Oprah was on the TV being clever and wise. Rinnie fell onto her bed, gasping for air, crying and scared to death.

———

At dinnertime, Mom and Dad told about their busy, but pleasant days. Rinnie tried to pay attention. When she dully recounted the saga of the boat ride without adding any of her usual wit and drama, they looked worried. She probably should've told them what happened *after* the boat ride. She honestly wanted to. But Rinnie didn't know which they'd think was worse, her encounter with Magda or the fact that she was at the house uninvited, snooping around, and right then, she didn't need a lecture. So when they asked what was wrong, she just said she had a headache and went to bed early.

Chapter 9

One Mixed-up Day

Rinnie knew Mom was trying to get her attention as they drove to the church the next morning for the girls' camp meeting. First, she tuned the radio to the oldies station. As a teenager, Rinnie knew it was sort of her *job* to at least groan about it, but she actually liked some of those songs. Most of the tapes they had at home were more from her parents' generation than hers, so she was used to them. When Rinnie didn't say anything, Mom gave her a quizzical look. Next, she tried the talk radio station and the Rush Limbaugh Show. Rinnie was used to that too. Dad listened to it all the time, so it didn't even make her flinch.

"Are you okay, Rinnie? Awfully quiet this morning," Mom finally asked, exasperated.

"I'm just real tired," Rinnie said softly. There wasn't time to get into a big discussion right then. She really *wanted* to tell Mom everything. It was eating her alive. The Magda episode baffled her, and that, added to all of her worries, made her feel nervous and nauseated. But it seemed like their desire for mother-daughter chats never landed at the same time.

When she needed to talk, Mom was busy
solving the problems of church people or
family, or doing housework. Sure, Rinnie was
usually there helping out but it was sort of
hard to talk about serious personal issues
when Mom was cleaning out the refrigerator,
which is what she'd been doing earlier that
morning. First came the throwing out of dead
leftovers. A smelly task. Then came the sorting
of the shriveled, gooey veggies from the
crisper. Rinnie was in charge of washing and
drying the shelves and bins as they became
emptied. The least favorite part was what
Rinnie called the march of the cottage cheese.
This involved lining up all the partially used-
up containers of cottage cheese, determining
which ones were rotten–usually half of them–
and dumping the moldy, stinky offenders
down the disposal. P.U.!

Mom used cottage cheese in almost everything:
lasagna, fruit salad, chip dip, and all kinds of
Jell-O recipes. The worst of these Mom called
Jell-O Surprise. Its ingredients could be leftovers of just about anything—fruit, nuts, or
even frozen vegetables, added to cottage
cheese of course—mixed with lime Jell-O.
Cottage cheese was also present in every
dinner she took to shut-ins, funerals, and
mothers of new babies. Rinnie could hardly
gag it down anymore.

It seemed that whenever they went to Costco,
they forgot if the cottage cheese they'd previ-
ously bought was still good, so they'd buy

more. As if that weren't bad enough, Mom always had her wash the old containers to be used in case they should ever run out of Tupperware. Mold could come in such pretty colors, but it still stunk to high heaven, so the march of the cottage cheese pretty much ended serious conversation.

On the other hand, there were times when Rinnie sensed that Mom felt like talking. She had a lot of responsibilities besides her family and often seemed emotionally drained. But Rinnie would get interrupted by phone calls from friends, and that Mom-chat opportunity passed. Or the boys would start fighting, or picking on her, so Mom's moments to relax and vent didn't come often.

Sometimes when they were driving around on errands they talked, like today when Mom asked, "Worrying about the stuff with Harold?" obviously trying to get a clue about what was going on in her daughter's head.

"Yeah," Rinnie said, but she wanted to yell, "You have *no* idea how much! Mom, I'm scared and I don't know what to do. I don't know who to trust. And I hate cottage cheese!" But suddenly there was the church parking lot and it was time to get out of the car.

"I'm gonna run to Costco, then drop some stuff off to Sister Bagley. See you in an hour or so."

Rinnie nodded and tried to smile.

After the camp planning meeting, Rinnie felt like a new person. It was so great to have something fun to look forward to. She chattered all the way home. Mom wanted to hear all the details about the food planning, what Rinnie needed to take, and she especially thought the secret-sister surprise thing sounded like it would be fun.

"So when do you find out who your secret sister is?"

"Well, the night before we leave, when we drop off all our camping stuff for inspection and to get packed in the trailer, we're gonna draw names. Then every day we will leave little treats and homemade gifts for that girl, under her pillow or in her shoe, or some sneaky place. It's all anonymous. It could even be as simple as a piece of gum on a cute note that says, 'Hope you have a great day!'"

"Then when do you tell her that you're her secret sister?"

"After prayer at the campfire the last night."

"Sounds neat. What else are they doing?"

Rinnie enthusiastically told her that the leaders were planning interesting ways for the girls to pass off the skills required to get a camp certification, like tying knots, first aid, nature study, scripture reading, and even the five-mile hike. None of it was going to be hard or boring. With so much to tell, the drive home went fast, and after she helped to carry in the groceries, which of course, included a fresh carton of cottage cheese, Rinnie went to meet Nick out by the tree house.

"Nick. Nick. Nick! How ya doin'?"

"Uh ... okay. You're pretty hyper. What'd they feed you at that meeting?"

Rinnie laughed, then repeated everything she'd told her mom about the camp meeting. She talked on and on, and ended with the part about singing around the campfire and how they were going to make s'mores, s'mores, s'mores, every night.

"Wow, sounds great. The secret sister thing is kind of sneaky, though."

"What are you talking about?"

"Well, it's a good way to make sure everyone gets along all week. No one's gonna be rude to anyone else just in case it might be her secret sister."

"Nicolas! It's not like that! It's to build camp spirit."

"Whatever—if you say so. Sounds like fun anyway. Makes me wish I could go."

"Oh, the girls would love that! But they never let cute guys go. Just dads." Rinnie froze, embarrassed. She couldn't believe she'd just blurted out that she thought Nick was cute. Okay, so he was, sort of. But still ... She blushed. "I think I'll go get some cookies for us. You can go up in the tree house and play with the cat, okay? Hope you're not allergic to cats like my brother, Squid, is. Anyway, I'll be right back."

Nick started to say he wasn't allergic, but she was already gone.

Rinnie was so flustered about what she'd said outside, she forgot that Nick wasn't very familiar with the cat. She hadn't warned him that Izabelle—the cat's original name—was nicknamed Miss Tizzy for good reason. She was nervous and extremely finicky. To Nick, she probably just seemed like a normal, very pregnant cat, who had made the tree house her new home. She especially liked the old couch cushion that the boys had brought up there to sit on. Tizzy wouldn't move off that for anyone! From the kitchen window, Rinnie could see that Nick had figured that out pretty fast and just sat down on the wooden floor.

What Rinnie didn't see was that after petting the cat for a couple of minutes, Nick looked around for something else to do, glanced over Rinnie's library book, and then started to investigate the air horn.

Rinnie was still in the kitchen when the loud blast sounded. Nick began yelling in pain. She grabbed the baggie of cookies and ran to his rescue.

"Nick, I'm so sorry. I'm so sorry. I forgot to tell you not to blast this horn around her," Rinnie apologized, as she knelt down to peel off the cat that was stuck like furry Velcro to his neck and face.

Nick was afraid to say anything until the beast was removed. Then he breathed a sigh of relief, as the cat crawled down the tree and waddled to the house.

"Are you alright?"

"No, I think I'm bleeding. Am I bleeding? "

"Well, just a little on the side of your nose. And maybe on your chin." Rinnie helped wipe the blood off with a napkin she'd stuffed in her pocket.

"My brothers used to tease her with that air horn when she was younger. I'm sorry that I didn't warn you. You aren't gonna sue us are you?"

Nick looked at her in mock fury. "I should! You should at least have to pay for the therapy I am gonna need,"

"Okay, I'll pay you with cookies. How many do you want?"

"How many have you got?"

Rinnie laughed. "You're so weird."

"Weird? Now I am really gonna need therapy!"

"No-no, I mean good weird—like funny weird—humorous."

"Oh, that's better—I guess—if you like making fun of people with cat pincushion scars on their faces." He looked down sadly.

Rinnie's smile faded. "Oh hey, I didn't mean— umm—I really am sorry about the cat."

Nick chuckled. "I know. I was kidding, relax!"

"You snot!"

"Yeah, most of the time. Anyway, that's what my mom says. So tell me, what the heck is a Hummel? It's been driving me nuts since yesterday wondering about it, and I don't have my computer hooked up so I couldn't check it."

"You have your own computer?"

"Well, yeah. Don't you?"

Rinnie wanted to yell, "Are you nuts? Our family's lucky to have one for the whole family to share, let alone me have one of my own!" But instead she deflected with, "Not yet, but I'm working on it." It wasn't a lie. She was working on it—sort of—working on wishing for one, and was hopeful that some year in the future she might actually have one. "Anyway," she continued, "Berta Hummel was born in the early 1900s. She was a talented artist and was especially good at drawing children. She later became a nun and took the name Sister Maria Innocentia. One day she was discovered by a man named Franz Goebel, who had a porcelain company. He just happened to be looking for an idea for a new line of porcelain figurines."

"Lucky timing for him—meeting her."

"Oh yeah. Anyway, Mr. Goebel made an agreement with the convent to make figurines based on Sister Maria Innocentia's drawings. They were a big success. Have been around for years."

"Okay, so your neighbor had some of these Hummel things."

"Yes, and each style is numbered and signed so they have become collector's items. Greta had twelve of them. Some of them were quite old and worth a bunch. Hundreds, even thousands of dollars."

"Wow! And she gave them to you? She must have liked you a lot!"

His words hit Rinnie very hard. Greta did like her a lot. Loved her actually—like a grandmother would. She looked away and blinked back a few tears. Nick appeared worried about her emotional reaction and tried to change the subject.

"So what happened to the nun?"

"She died when she was only thirty-seven," Rinnie sighed. "But all of the Hummels they have made since then follow her same style ideas and are signed by Goebel and numbered."

"Well, that's something at least," Nick added, uneasily, not knowing what else to say. He stood up and looked out over the lake. "Wow, this is an incredible view!"

Rinnie wiped her eyes, sniffled, then joined him at the railing. "I know. I love living here. The house is old, but we're planning to remodel someday. In the meantime we get to look out at this. That is, until your dad changes everything. I really shouldn't be talking to you, ya know."

"Why?"

"Because your dad's building all those big houses. Gonna ruin our lake!"

"No it won't. It'll be better in the long run."

Rinnie chuckled sarcastically. "How do you figure that? Going from eight houses spread over two miles to thirty or more? Is that better?"

"Sure. New roads. New boat launches."

"But just for the people who live there."

"Still, it could have been worse," Nick defended. "Look, my dad's selling twenty big lots around Raven Cove Lake. If Mr. Chase had bought it, he planned to sell fifty tiny lots and rename it Chase Landing. Which would you rather have?"

"Neither!"

"I know. But people want places to build a home. Some want a place where they can have a floatplane."

"Oh yes, those poor deprived floatplane people!"

Nicolas frowned. "Why shouldn't people have floatplanes if they want them? Alaska has more floatplanes per capita than any other state."

"I know that!" Now she was getting annoyed.

"Okay, so if they have a floatplane, why shouldn't they be able to build a house by a lake?"

Rinnie had no good answer for that. She could actually see that there were two sides to the argument. She just didn't like all the changes that were coming in her backyard. The concern that the lake might be ruined made her unreasonable.

"So?" Nick continued. "Which would you choose if you had to?"

"Which what? Oh—okay, the twenty lots. It might not seem as crowded. But still, many people just gave up and sold out instead of staying put and making them build the new houses around them."

"Who told you that?"

"Well, there were a lot of old-timers around here. They must have felt pressured."

"That's just stupid gossip. They sold because they wanted to. Mostly their homes were old and falling apart. They had a chance to get some money, get something new to live in closer to town or do some traveling. They got a good price for their land; I have seen some of the papers—had to help file a bunch of them. People didn't get ripped off at all!"

Nicolas was obviously biased in his opinion, thought Rinnie, but at least he seemed to care. Maybe if his dad was as concerned as Nick was, and not just gung-ho to bulldoze the neighborhood it would be okay, and she would eventually get used to it. She tried to lighten the mood a bit.

"Well, at least Mr. Moore's place will still be around, and we can still have access to the lake and not get our view blocked."

"Yeah, until next fall when they're ready to knock down the rest of the old houses on his side of the lake, and stake out new lots."

"What? No! Harold Moore will never sell that place. He wants to live there until he dies, and then maybe it could be sold."

"Uh—Rinnie," he hesitated. "I hate to tell you this, but he already signed the property papers."

Rinnie's mouth fell open. "No way! I know him. He loves that place!"

"Sorry. I thought you knew."

"No! This can't be right. You must've misunderstood. Maybe you're thinking of the Hastings house down around the corner."

Nick shook his head sympathetically.

"Well, I still don't believe it."

Nick apologetically said. "I've seen the papers, Rinnie. I've heard Dad talking about it with the real estate guy. He's not my dad's favorite person to work with, but he said the papers were all in order."

"Then all I can say is, somebody ripped Harold Moore off! Because there is no way this can be real. Maybe he was having a bad day. He hasn't been himself lately. Remember, I told you that he seemed different? Maybe they came and tricked him into signing!"

"No way! My dad doesn't do business like that!" Nick defended loudly. "You just can't face the truth."

"Yeah? And maybe you can't tell the truth!" Rinnie shouted back. Saying those words to Nick made her feel sick inside, and she was about to apologize when he yelled back.

"Well maybe you are just jealous that you can't afford a new house and if they put up a fence, you won't be able to even get near your precious lake!"

Rinnie gasped. Hot tears of anger welled up in

her eyes. Her face burned red. Nick looked like someone had hit him in the stomach too. They stared at each other, wishing they'd never started the argument, helpless to know what to say next to make the horrible moment fade away.

"Sounds like you two need to take a break." Ruth Cumberland called out firmly from the back porch where she stood drying her hands on a dishcloth. "Dinnertime, Rinnie. Come set the table, please. Good night, Nick"

Nick nodded and left. He was halfway down the rope ladder before he spoke again. "Night, Rinnie," he said softly.

"Bye," was all she could manage.

Chapter 10

Harold's Homecoming

Harold Moore came home on Saturday. Rinnie and her mother took dinner down to him and Magda. He was sitting outside in his heavy wooden lawn chair, enjoying the evening sights and sounds. Balancing herself on a crutch dramatically, Magda met them on the porch. She seemed oh, so grateful for lasagna, Jell-O fruit salad and rolls, and thrilled with the brownies. It was oh, so phony. Rinnie didn't stay to listen. She helped hand the food over, then went to visit with Mr. Moore. He seemed better in some ways, but he didn't remember a lot about what had taken place a few days earlier.

"Well, I'm just glad you're okay now," Rinnie smiled and gave him a soft hug. "Me and my friend Nick got the canoe in for you."

"The canoe was out?"

"Yeah, but it's okay. It's all tied up just fine now."

"That's nice."

Rinnie nearly cried. Harold was there, but

not there. Magda came walking around the corner with Ruth Cumberland. "These nice neighbors brought us a lovely dinner," Magda gushed. "Come in now, and let's eat it before it gets cold."

It sounded so fake Rinnie about gagged. Still she helped Mom carefully lift Harold by the arms and walk him slowly into the house.

"We brought you some lasagna, Harold," Ruth raised her voice a bit, as if the old man was deaf as well as partially blind. "I made you some rolls and brownies too. I used the recipes Greta gave me. Thought you might like that."

"Oh, that's so kind of you. Greta would be so pleased. Thank you," Mr. Moore said, getting tears in his eyes. He let them each give him a hug. Magda didn't seem to appreciate this little display of affection, and appeared to be glad when the Cumberlands left a few minutes later.

"That went well," Rinnie's mom sighed, as they walked home.

"I hope she lets him eat it."

"Oh, she will. Why wouldn't she?"

"Mom! You saw how thin and pale he was! And the house is not the same. It feels horrible and creepy to me. Something bad's going on there. Can't you feel it?"

"Rinnie, sometimes a feeling is just a feeling."

"What about the still, small voice of warning in your head that they talk about at church? Or the go-with-your-gut sense like Oprah says?"

Ruth chuckled at the Oprah part, then said, "Rinnie, there's also imagination, and not saying things about people that aren't true."

"What about isolation, and controlling behavior that are warning signs of abuse like Oprah talked about too."

"Yes, Rinnie, but we have to be careful."

Rinnie shook her head sadly, "Well, I just hope while we're being careful that nothing else bad happens to Harold Moore."

They walked in silence the rest of the way to the house. Rinnie spent the rest of the night in her room.

Chapter 11

Sometimes a Feeling...

The question on Rinnie's mind when she went to church on Sunday was about feelings. When *was* a feeling a prompting or a warning and not an imagined worry? Rinnie pondered this all through the meetings. She finally ended up praying silently that *something* definite would happen that would make the answer to the Harold Moore dilemma obvious, bring it out into the open before it was too late.

When Rinnie and her mom delivered dinner Sunday night, Magda's thank you was far less dramatic. "Please don't worry about bringing it again," she said. "Harold and I are doing fine."

Harold didn't look fine. He sat motionless in his old recliner and only nodded when Ruth and Rinnie greeted him. The inhospitable silence was very awkward, so the Cumberlands didn't stay long.

"Okay... well, we'll just run along then," Ruth said.

"Say good-bye to the ladies, Harold," Magda prompted him.

He nodded. "Can Rinnie stay for a minute, please?" he asked.

"Sure!" she answered joyfully, thinking he might want her to read to him.

After her mother was gone. Harold reached down by the side of his chair, picked up a small brown bag and handed it to her. When she opened it, she was happily surprised to see the tiniest of Greta's Hummels. It was the one called "Bookworm," a favorite of Rinnie's.

"You forgot one," Harold said, scowling.

"What do you mean?"

"Magda said you broke in while we were gone and took all the others, but since this one was in my room, I guess you missed it. You might as well take it now,"

Rinnie was stunned! "That's not true! I would never break in. I would never need to!" The whole thing was absurd! Her family had had an extra key to the Moore house for almost three years, in case of an emergency.

Harold knew this; still he didn't seem to hear her trying to explain. "Take the dang thing and put it with the others. They were supposed to come to you eventually anyway. Too bad you couldn't wait. But one thing, I *do* want the records you stole returned immediately. I can still get some enjoyment from them."

"Records? You think I took your records?"
Rinnie repeated, numb.

"Magda wanted me to call the police and
report it, but I told her Greta wouldn't be
happy with that. I won't tell your parents if
you bring the records back tomorrow. They're
good people. They don't need that kind of
embarrassment."

"Harold, I didn't steal anything from you. I
wouldn't do that. You're like family to me!"
Rinnie protested, starting to cry.

"See? I told you. She lies and denies!" Magda
said, coming into the living room.

"No!" Rinnie shook her head.

Harold waved his hand, weakly dismissing her.
"Take the Hummel, but bring back the records.
Then don't come back again."

A very pleased look spread across Magda's
face, as Rinnie ran from the house, clutching
the precious porcelain figurine to her heart.

Overwhelmed and dejected, Rinnie had trouble
saying her prayers at bedtime. This couldn't be
the answer she was looking for, could it? Suddenly she got a warm, calm feeling and knew
that it was important for her not to lose faith,
or give up hope.

Chapter 12

The Wrong Write

Rinnie sat on her sleeping bag thumbing through the many love letters that Greta and Harold had exchanged in their long courtship. The letters represented years of devotion. Rinnie knew Greta would be heart-broken to see Harold the way he was now. He was like a broken-down stranger. It made Rinnie ache inside almost as badly as when Greta died—a heavy kind of hurting that makes it hard to even cry. In this daze she didn't even hear Nick Nedders coming up the path. She nearly jumped out of her skin when he asked, "Can I come up?"

Jumping to her feet, she panted, "You scared me to death!"

"Sorry," Nick said, as he made his way to the top of the swaying rope ladder.

Rinnie stood with her back to the railing. "So— are you okay?"

"Not really. I had this new friend and we got into a big fight and I was afraid that she wouldn't ever talk to me again."

"She feels worse than you do, trust me," Rinnie said, with a shy smile. "Hey—I'm really sorry."

"Me too."

Rinnie turned around and stared over the rail down to the lawn. "I decided if you didn't come back I'd just add it to the list of rotten things that have happened in the last few days, and accept the fact that my life is basically going to be a horrible nightmare from now on."

Nick put his hand on her shoulder and said in a silly, gruff voice, "Okay, tell Uncle Nick about all the horrible things that have been happening to you."

Rinnie reached into a small tissue-padded box, handed him the little Hummel that Mr. Moore had sent her home with, and told him the accusation story.

"Wow, that's bad! Did you tell your parents?"

"Yeah."

"What did they say?"

"They said, Harold's obviously not mentally well, and I shouldn't go there anymore."

"Probably a good idea, but—man! That stinks!"

"Yup. It totally stinks!"

Nick looked sad. "Rinnie, I don't want to add

to your troubles, but I've gotta tell you something. Sunday, for some reason, I had this feeling that I needed to show you this paper. Not to be mean, just to let you know, okay?"

"Okay."

Nick unfolded two full-size pieces of paper that he'd taken from his pocket and held them out for her to see. "It's called an earnest money. My dad said I could show you this copy."

Glancing down at the paper, Rinnie saw that the property address listed was that of Harold Moore. A sick feeling twisted in her stomach as she scanned the pages. Rinnie's worst fears were about to be confirmed, when her gaze reached the signature line on the bottom of the second page. Harold Moore's signature had never looked so good. There it was, the answer to her prayer. "Nick, I could kiss you!"

"What?"

"Well, I could hug you anyway. This is not Harold's signature."

"It *has* to be; it's been notarized."

"I don't know about that. Obviously there's a problem. Didn't you say that your dad was unhappy with his real estate guy?"

"Yeah?"

"Well, it looks like he has reason to be! I

promise you that I've seen Harold Moore's writing enough to know that he couldn't write this neatly when he could see everything, let alone now that he's going blind. There's no way he signed this!"

"You're sure?"

"Absolutely!"

"And you can prove it?"

"Only about two hundred times," Rinnie said, ecstatically, picking up the box of Harold-Greta love letters.

"Then who would be forging his signature?"

Rinnie nodded and smiled a very big smile. "Two guesses!"

"Are you serious? You think Magda would risk going to jail, and someone else would be dumb enough to risk their career by okaying a fake signature?"

"It's possible. Someone might do it for a lot of money."

"Where would Magda get that kind of money?"

Rinnie thought for a moment, then held up the littlest Hummel that Harold had insisted she take. "Like I said, some of these are very rare. Eleven of them are missing."

"How could she think she'd get away with it?"

"Well, if he'd drowned in the lake, and I'd never met you, she *would* have gotten away with it."

"I think my dad needs to call your folks." Rinnie smiled again. "Uh, yeah."

After Mr. James Nedder talked to Bill Cumberland, they called a detective friend of Bill's from the police department who was very interested in the whole story.

Chapter 13

Hometown Tourists

The morning before Rinnie's brothers came home, her dad and two other scout dads left in a convoy on an eight-hour drive to rendezvous with the returning troop, to haul boys and equipment home. They wouldn't be back until tomorrow. Rinnie and her mom had more interesting plans, and drove to downtown Anchorage to play tourist.

They dressed cute, tied sweaters around their waists, and wore sunglasses so they could blend in with the hundreds of tourists that milled through the souvenir shops and museums. They took an old camera with no film in it, and pretended to take endless snapshots of: flowering lobelia baskets that hung from lampposts all along the streets, a horse-drawn carriage, other tourists and of course, anyone who looked even remotely Alaskan. They browsed through racks of postcards, T-shirts, key chains, and coffee mugs that had "ALASKA" proudly printed across them. They saw other things to buy such as ivory carvings, gold nugget jewelry, and huge wire mosquitoes whose bodies were made out of petrified moose droppings.

"Talk about a gag gift!" Rinnie said, making a gagging motion.

"Don't you have anyone on your list that you would like to send petrified moose droppings too?"

"Oh sure, but since I have only five dollars, I may have to settle for fresh ones that were left in our front yard."

They'd laughed at that, but the silliest moment came when Ruth Cumberland stood her daughter in front of a mirror and told her to close her eyes.

"Now open them," she giggled.

There stood Rinnie with a moose antler hat on.

"It's the closest thing to Mickey Mouse ears I could find."

"Well, slap my back and call me Bullwinkle!"

"Maybe we should buy it."

"Or not!" Rinnie shook her head.

They were still talking about it a few minutes later when they stopped to buy the luncheon special from a gourmet hot dog vendor. They each got a reindeer sausage, a bag of chips and a can of pop for $4.50.

On their way home, they stopped at McDonald's

for a fifty-cent ice cream cone. As they sat in the parking lot eating, Rinnie's mom said, "See, you can have fun in Alaska without spending a lot of money. No wonder the tourists enjoy it!"

"Yeah, and it was fun just hanging out together."

"Thanks. That's a nice thing to say. I've been worried a lot about you lately. Are you okay, honey?"

Rinnie got a still, small nudge. "Talk to her," it urged. She took a deep breath and let it all out. "It's just that I feel so weird. I've got all this *stuff* going on. It's driving me nuts! My moods go wild. I'm happy, then I'm sad. I get a lot of weird thoughts. And sometimes I even have a hard time praying. And this thing about Disneyland—sometimes I just get jealous and restless and want dumb stuff." A year's worth of fears, questions, and feelings poured out of her. She cried most of the way through it.

Her mother cried some too. "I wish you'd talked to me sooner instead of letting things build up so long. Not that I have all the answers. But I do know it helps to talk through it at times, so you don't feel like you're struggling alone."

"You have too many other people's problems to solve."

"Rinnie—look at me. You're number one to me. Don't ever doubt it. When you need me, I will drop everything else. You just have to let me in!"

Rinnie leaned across the seat, put her head on her mother's shoulder and sobbed.

A few minutes later, they drove through the McDonald's drive-up again, and ordered two cups of ice water and some extra napkins so they could blow their noses. The look on the girl's face when they picked up their order was so strange that they burst out laughing.

When they arrived home, there was a message from Bill's detective friend. Harold Moore had been removed that morning from Magda's care, with the State taking temporary guardianship pending an investigation and a mental evaluation.

"Magda's the one who needs the mental evaluation. She's a wacko!" Rinnie remarked.

"I don't know if she's crazy. Maybe just unkind, so let's be careful what we say about her."

"Mom, you don't know her like I do." Rinnie felt flustered, and finally told about the crutch incident and the threats by the shed. "She shoved her face into mine and yelled at me to mind my own business—or else!"

"She did what?"

"And she was pushing me back against the door until I could barely breathe! I'm tellin' you, Mom, it was so scary!"

"You should have told me right away, honey!"

"I know. I'm sorry! But you were so busy, and I was afraid you'd be mad at me."

"No way. I'd have marched down there and ripped her hair out!"

"Really?"

"Absolutely! You shouldn't have been snooping around uninvited, but still, she's supposed to be a rational adult, not a—a..."

"Maniac?"

"Exactly!"

"Thank heavens Rascal bit her and I got away."

"She must've been afraid that someone would find out how poorly she was treating Harold. She knew it was wrong."

"Exactly!" Rinnie echoed.

"Well, under the circumstances, I don't think you should sleep out in the tree house alone tonight."

"You wanna sleep out there with me?"

"No. How about you sleeping in my room with me, and we'll make popcorn and watch *Ever After.*

"It's a date!" Rinnie said, with a big, wide grin.

Chapter 14

Rascal's Rescue

About 4 a.m. Rinnie was awakened by an odd yelping sound. She listened for a minute, not wanting to wake up and get out of her mother's cozy, warm bed. It was probably a magpie. Still, the yipping became more intense and Rinnie focused her attention on it. She slipped quietly out of bed and went into Mom and Dad's bathroom.

Through the window screen the sound became clearer. It was Rascal! But it wasn't coming from under the deck, his newest place of residence. It was farther down the yard than that.

"Mom," Rinnie whispered. "I think Rascal's in trouble. I'm gonna look in the bushes by the tree house."

"Hmm?" Mom mumbled, sleepily. "Don't go very far, honey."

"Okay." Rinnie stopped in her room to get her slippers and Henley sweater. Next she grabbed a piece of bread, in case she needed something to coax the poor dog with. Absentmindedly, she started to eat the bread as she walked across the back lawn. The crisp Alaska morning air nipped at her cheeks and nose, fully waking her up. She pulled the sweater over her pajamas and fastened the buttons— any extra warmth was appreciated.

The farther away from the house she got, the more Rinnie realized that Rascal was not stuck in the bushes out back. In a moment it was obvious that he was trapped in Harold's shed again. Rinnie decided to sneak down there and let him loose. She wasn't really afraid of Magda, now that people had become aware of her deception and trickery. Still she didn't trust the woman and hoped she was asleep. That hope faded fast.

The lights were on in the house. From the look of things in the carport, Magda was loading up her rusty old Suburban, getting ready to leave. The problem was that most of the things she was loading belonged to Harold Moore. Rinnie could see an open box sitting on the tailgate next to a ball of twine, some clear packing tape and Harold's life-saving pocketknife. Obviously, Magda hadn't been in Alaska long enough to discover the wonders of duct tape. A crutch was lying on the ground. Apparently Magda didn't need it anymore to get around. Hmm— Magda at full speed might be a problem.

Rinnie wasn't sure what to do. She knew she should call the police, but Rascal sounded so miserable, and she was afraid of what Magda might do to him before she left, out of spite. Rinnie still didn't get a good go-ahead feeling, but decided to set Rascal free, then hightail it home to call 911. "Heaven help me!" she whispered and ran to the shed.

Rinnie found the dog tied to Harold's old lawn mower and tangled up around it in the corner of the shed. She gave him what was left of the bread to quiet him down. That didn't last long. The more she succeeded in untangling him, the more grateful he was—yipping and licking her face. What a racket he made! Finally Rinnie got Rascal loose and headed for the shed door. Magda opened it.

"You!" she snarled, as startled to see Rinnie as Rinnie was to see her. Magda grabbed a heavy old canoe paddle and stood like a barricade between Rinnie and the door. "Stupid little brat! You just don't learn, do you? Just like this dumb dog! I've chased him away. I've starved him away. I've beaten him away. But he still comes back."

Magda raised the paddle as though she was ready to strike Rascal again. The dog growled but cowered. Rinnie knelt down and protectively wrapped her arms around him.

This made Magda laugh. "You think you can save him? Who's going to save you? I have nothing left to lose. You've seen to that. Someone has to pay!"

Rinnie's horrified glance darted to the paddle.

"Oh, and yes, you and your little friend guessed

right. The oars were *not* in the boat. It's not like Harold could have used them. But I can!" She jabbed the oar toward her captives and laughed when they dodged out of the way.

Rinnie's mind reeled in fear, but she knew she had to do something—say something—to give herself more time to think.

"You starved a little dog? Whoa! That must make you feel big and tough!" The disgusted, sarcastic words flew out of her mouth. Why she'd said that Rinnie wasn't sure, but it worked. For a moment she'd actually shut Magda up, so she went for it. "And when you succeeded in starving Rascal, you decided to starve Harold too, didn't you? No wonder he's skinny!"

Magda smirked. "Almost figured it out, didn't you? But not quite. The dog had to go because he didn't like me and was interfering. It made Harold not trust me. With him out of the house—and no visitors—it was easy to give the old guy a little less food every day, stop giving him his medicine and watch his old brain start to fog up."

"You witch! Why would you pick on Harold? He never did anything to you."

Magda didn't even flinch at the witch comment. She just smiled that phony mannequin smile and said, "Harold was so sad. He wanted to go to heaven and be with his beloved Greta. I tried to help him. Helped him into that boat— all nice and groggy— figured he'd

fall into the water eventually and slip peace-
fully away. You were the one who spoiled it
for him. I was just following Greta's example
of compassion."

"You're nothing like Greta! She was beautiful.
She was wonderful."

"She was a liar and a cheat!" Magda's eyes
narrowed—her face twisted into a bitter, poi-
sonous grimace. "Good old Greta! The big
sister. The pretty one. When I was little, she
told me stories about her plan to marry a rich
man, get his money and leave. We were going
to travel around Europe. But she fell in love
with a poor man—in Alaska of all places—and
that was that. She even became a Christian,"
Magda spat the word out in disgust. "She
wanted me to come live here too. To be
happy. I was already happy—happily waiting
for the time I could get even. Get what was
owed to me. Take anything that was left and
destroy the rest."

Rinnie's eyes widened in terror; still her mind
searched for calm. "Okay, so you've got everything—go!"

"I have some unfinished business to attend to."
Magda wedged the oar across the door,
reached into her jacket and pulled out the
pocketknife. "They're coming back today to
investigate. We might as well give them something good to investigate, right?"

"You're crazy!" Rinnie gasped. Her fear seemed

to give Magda pleasure. "You'll never get away with it. They'll find me."

"Will they? Does your mother even know where you are now? Does she even know where to look?"

A sick realization hit Rinnie. Her mother had no idea where she was. It was a horrible, helpless feeling.

"By the time they find your stinking bones, I'll be long gone. You know how big Alaska is. I may even go to Canada. I hear they have some lovely hot springs." Magda started to back Rinnie up into the corner. "Say hi to Greta for me!"

In a flash, Rascal jumped up and bit Magda's hand. She dropped the knife. With that distraction, Rinnie jumped behind the old mower and pushed it into Magda, who fell backward onto some boxes. Rinnie moved the oar and dashed out the door, but she didn't get far.

Magda caught hold of the bottom of her sweater and began reeling her back into the shed. Rinnie strained forward as hard as she could. Frantically she tore at the buttons to loosen them. It was impossible! Magda pulled back so hard that the sweater crept up Rinnie's throat choking her. What could she do? Her slippers didn't help—there wasn't any tread for traction. She started to slide back into the shed. Then in her mind, Rinnie heard the words—peel it off!

Rinnie began to panic. Peel it off?

Suddenly a calm wave flooded her mind. She turned from desperate to determined. Grabbing the bottom of her sweater with all her strength, Rinnie forced it up over her stomach, past her shoulders and above her face. Her head tipped back so sharply, she was afraid her neck would crack. Then—zing! The sweater popped up over her head and flipped into Magda's face, stinging her with a button. Rinnie fell forward, but soon was on her feet again.

Madga cursed. Rinnie ran.

"Go, go!" she yelled to Rascal, and he did, in exactly the same direction as Rinnie, and just as scared. They crossed the road but when Rinnie jumped the ditch her feet tripped over Rascal and she fell again. One of her slippers came off, but she couldn't stop for it. They started zig-zagging up the hill. She had to get home—fast!

Amazingly, Magda was hot on her trail. Adrenaline and anger had given the woman a renewed burst of energy—the distance between them was closing! Rascal's canine courage resurfaced and he doubled back to try to stop Magda along the way. She booted him with her splinted foot and he went yelping off into the bushes.

Reaching the top of the hill, Rinnie had to make a quick decision. She might not make it across the lawn without slipping on the damp grass, and with this madwoman behind her, she couldn't risk getting caught. Her best bet was to get out of Magda's reach as fast as possible. Rinnie grabbed the wobbly rope ladder and started climbing for the tree house. She was up about four rungs when Magda grabbed her slippered foot. Rinnie kicked and kicked until the slipper came off, then kept going. Two more rungs! Just two more rungs, she told herself.

As Rinnie threw herself past the last rung, she felt the rope pull down heavy. Magda was coming up after her! Until this moment Rinnie had never been glad that the rope ladder was unsteady. Thank heavens! It'd take Magda a few extra seconds to climb it, and Rinnie needed the time.

Scrambling across the wood planks, she pulled the cushion with Miss Tizzy on it closer to the ladder. "Sorry Tizzy!" Rinnie cried out. Then she pointed the air horn toward the house and blared it, screaming as loud as she could.

Immediately the crazed cat jumped onto the enraged woman's face as it emerged over the top ladder rung. She shrieked and fell backward into the bushes below.

Ruth Cumberland appeared seconds later, a broom raised high over her head. "Don't you move a muscle, lady, or I'll let you have it. And if you hurt my cat, you're gonna get it anyway."

Chapter 15

Tizzy's Revenge

After the police took Magda out of the bushes, the EMTs wheeled her away again but handcuffed to the gurney this time. It took them longer than planned because Rascal kept trying to jump on the gurney and bite her. Now that his tormentor was restrained, Rascal was fearless. Enraged, Magda ranted on and on. Her story had an absurd logic. She'd done nothing wrong. Her sister *owed* her from a long time ago. Why shouldn't Magda collect what was left?

Rinnie felt overwhelmed just listening to all the nonsense from a distance, as she talked to the police on the back deck. Mom stood close by, calming the trembling Tizzy. When everyone had left, Rinnie went into the house and collapsed onto the couch. She didn't wake up until noon, when her boisterous brothers bolted from the car and started dragging their smelly scout gear into the garage.

Ruth Cumberland looked out the curtains, "Well, they're home. There goes the peace and quiet," she chuckled.

"Peace and quiet?" Rinnie asked, sarcastically, and opened one eye.

Mom tousled Rinnie's hair and went back into the kitchen to finish making lasagna for the Carson family, to help out with dinner, since Sister Carson just had a new baby. "We've had some interesting phone calls while you were asleep," she called out. "One was from Nick. He said to tell you that his mom is coming up to check out Alaska, and maybe try living here for a year."

"Cool!"

"Are you hungry?"

"Sure. What've we got?" Rinnie asked, staggering sleepily into the kitchen.

"There's Jell-O surprise."

"Uhh—no thanks. So, what were the other phone calls?"

"Well, apparently now that Harold is getting fed right, and receiving the proper medication, his mental state is becoming much clearer. If he keeps improving, he may be able to come home in a week or so."

"Wow, that's great!"

"He also said to tell us he'd like a visit. Wondered why his Rinnie-girl hasn't been around to read him the newspaper for such a long time."

Tears of relief filled Rinnie's eyes. "Now that's the Harold Moore we all know and love. What in the world was Magda giving to him, Mom?"

"Hardly anything— little food, none of his medicine. No wonder he was so out of it. They're bound to add abuse of the elderly to her theft and forgery charges. Luckily she hadn't sold everything of Harold's yet. They found a bunch of things packed in the car; the rest of his pocketknives, even some of the Hummels."

"Really?" Rinnie cried out, excitedly.

"Thanks to you, she didn't get away with anything else. But oh Rinnie, that was so dangerous!"

"I know Mom. It all happened so fast." Rinnie started to tear up, and went for a hug. All the frightening emotions of the day's events came flooding out.

Ruth Cumberland wrapped her arms around her daughter. "Maybe tomorrow we can make cookies again and take some to Harold. He might even like to meet Nick."

Rinnie's cheeks turned pink, and she smiled shyly.

"Oh, and two more phone calls came in."

"What were they about?"

"Well, it seems that since your story ran in the newspaper, they have received several letters and cards for you. There was also an offer from a local travel agency. They want to know if you'd like a buy-one-get-one-free plane ticket?"

"Really? Where to?"

"Disneyland!"

Rinnie and her mother burst out laughing.

———•———

"What a lazy bum!" Squid accused when he came in the door a few minutes later, seeing that Rinnie was still in her pajamas. "We've been up for hours, driving home."

"Rinnie's been up too," their mother chimed in. "She's been saving trapped animals and battling crazy people."

"Really?" Bill Cumberland asked, concerned and bewildered.

Yup," Mom said, and nodded toward the back-yard where yellow police tape could be seen dangling from the tree house and bushes be-low. "Oh ... and from now on, that air horn is *not* to come within a hundred yards of my cat!"

The boys barely heard her. In a second they were whooping and hollering their way out there, leaving the back door wide open. To them, yellow police tape meant, come on in!

"Boys!" Dad called out, and went after them, but they were already reclaiming their territory.

"Pink curtains!" Squid yelled.

A few seconds later, the old towels came sail-ing out through the window and landed clum-sily on the lawn like two flopping flamingos.

"Oh well, it looked nicer for a while," Rinnie shrugged. She held the strainer over the sink so her mother could drain the lasagna noodles.

Mom chuckled and shook her head.

Squid suddenly sneezed loudly, and Russell yelled, "Mom, your dang cat's up here having kittens!"

"Kittens? Right now?" Rinnie squealed.

Mom took hold of the strainer. "You'd better go check on Tizzy," she said, with a wink.

That was the only encouragement Rinnie needed. "Thanks, Mom!" she squealed again, and raced out to the tree house, pajamas and all.

Her brothers started to protest as Rinnie climbed up the rope ladder. "Hey, you can't come up here, this is a guy's place."

"Mom!" they called out in dismay.

"Things change, boys. Get used to it," Mom hollered back, as she reached for the cottage cheese.

Another book by Halene Petersen Dahlstrom

Christmas Connections:
Miracles—one good deed at a time

A holiday novel of hope, love, and spiritual connection to be enjoyed by young and old, again and again.

Halene is available to speak to school, community or church groups.

For more information contact:
Halene Dahlstrom at halenepd@yahoo.com, or Publication Consultants at www.alaskabooks.biz.